MW00714531

Frozen Heart

Annabelle Blume

The characters and events in this book are fictitious. Any similarity to real persons, living or dead, places, or events is coincidental and not intended by the author.

If you purchase this book without a cover you should be aware that this book may have been stolen property and reported as "unsold and destroyed" to the publisher. In such case the author has not received any payment for this "stripped book."

Frozen Heart

Copyright © 2012 Annabelle Blume

All rights reserved.

Paperback ISBN: 978-0-9851483-5-5

ePub ISBN: 978-0-9851483-6-2

Inkspell Publishing

18, Scott Court, C-4

Ridgefield Park

07660 NJ

Edited By Melissa Keir.

Cover art By Najla Qamber

You can visit us at www.inkspellpublishing.com

This book, or parts thereof, may not be reproduced in any form without permission. The copying, scanning, uploading, and distribution of this book via the internet or via any other means without the permission of the publisher is illegal and punishable by law. Please purchase only authorized electronic or print editions, and do not participate in or encourage piracy of copyrighted materials. Your support of the author's rights is appreciated.

ACKNOWLEDGMENTS

Amy and Dee – I couldn't have done it without you.

M5 – thanks for the inspiration

ANNABELLE BLUME

DEDICATION

For Michael, with love

ANNABELLE BLUME

CHAPTER ONE
Morning Light

I pressed my hands against the heated ceramic of my mug in hopes of stealing some of its warmth. The cold had burrowed so deep into my bones that the burn of the smooth surface barely registered. I usually dismissed the intense chill in my body as a consequence of the never-ending snow and ice that surrounded me, but sometimes an errant thought snuck into my head and left me wondering if it might be something more.

It had been three months since I'd seen another human being out here in the frozen tundra. Three months since my last trip to the Collective, my last interaction with another actual person. Whether we were about to welcome a friend or fight off an intruder currently depended on the identity of the prowler lurking around the exterior of our meager shelter. More shuffling noises from outside the cabin forced me to still my breathing in an effort to distinguish the source.

Another scrape and drag echoed. My heart picked up an extra beat, but I willed my body to be still and silent. I surveyed Tonk and Tilo's reaction to the stimuli. If we were dealing with a human, or worse yet, a Reaper, they'd let me know. Their thick-coated ears tilted, following the sounds around the perimeter of our home. The low rumble in Tonk's chest meant our luck hadn't run out. With a satisfied smile, I calmed my nerves before I got ready to pounce.

I left my tea at the small table near the glowing coils of my hearth, giddy at our good fortune. It wasn't every day that dinner brought itself to our table. I grabbed my spear and poised for the kill. Tonk and Tilo readied themselves on each side of the access door. A menacing snort from the beast forced air through the deteriorating seams of the entrance. I hit the access button and sized up the ferocious beast as it came into view.

Snarling and frothing at the mouth from disease or from dehydration, or maybe both, it opened its huge mouth and unsheathed two long fangs. Spots of brown mottled its murky grey-green fur, which would make it nearly imperceptible in the thicker portions of the forest. It stood to its full height for only a second before I thrust my spear into its chest, right through the heart. The fatal wound brought its massive form to the ground. Tilo and Tonk hauled in our game and I shut the access door as quickly as possible. The animal was near starvation, its belly hollow and rib cage prominent through its heavy fur.

A flicker of wonder buzzed across my thoughts at the origin of this species. A predatory cat of some sort, maybe, before man and science got their hands on its gene pool. Funny how, initially, cloning seemed like the obvious answer to the increasing list of extinct species. But once they got started, the far-reaching experiments of egotistical scientists could not be curtailed. I thanked the two moons that it had never occurred to those God-complex fiends to make the flesh poisonous. What would have been left for us then?

I made quick work of cleaning and dressing our boon. The fur, though coarse and unattractive, would make for a good trade in the Collective. I would probably have enough to line my boots and fashion a vest, too. The beast's large size meant I could keep some for myself as well. The claws would serve as great spear tips, and the meat, though meager, would serve the dogs and me for a month, if I rationed it carefully.

I checked my supplies, disappointed to find only a small mound of salt at the bottom of my canister. I'd have to prepare the furs today and head out for the Collective in the morning. I could bury some of the meat in a snow pack, but the rest would need to be salted and dried as soon as possible.

"T and T?" I tossed some entrails their way. They yelped and danced in excitement, taking their pieces to different corners before devouring the first bites of flesh they'd had in weeks. Rice porridge and toasted lentils kept us fed, but left us hungry for more. "We're headed out with the first spot of the sun tomorrow. You boys up for it?" Tilo yipped but Tonk ignored me, solely concentrated on cleaning his massive paws of any tasty remnants. "All right then, I'm gonna get the sled pack ready. You two, be good, now."

***

The round edge of the second moon had snuck onto the horizon before I had the fur sectioned and the sled ready for our two days of travel. In the short time I'd had my gloves off to secure the twine, my fingers had grown numb. Satisfied with the light load, I blew into my hands and considered making a new set of gloves instead of lining my boots. I shrugged to myself, figuring I'd wait and see what I had left after I made my vest.

Heading back in, I noticed the trail of blood that had escaped the beast's wound before I got it into the tub. It had gone sticky, trapped in a state between freezing solid and staying liquid on the permanently hard and icy ground. Though the solar-powered coils, strategically mounted around the one-room living quarters, warmed the air inside the cabin, there were some things about an Ice Age you couldn't combat in the wild. I needed to use some of the water reserve to wash off the mess. Wouldn't want to risk inviting more trouble now that the darkness was upon us.

The boys were curled up near each other on their fur-covered mats in front of the hearth, sleeping soundly with full bellies and their hunting instincts sated. I flipped on the radio transmitter to keep me company while I cleaned the mess from our kill. Transmissions from the Outlier network were few and far between, only vital information about new laws and regulations or reports of those who were reaped back into the Collective camps, but tonight there was nothing to be heard. I let the shadowy static fill the room in the hope that someone would reach out anyway. Even though both moons were strong and bright, the night felt darker than it had in some time.

The frame of the cot groaned and protested at my restless and fidget-filled unease. Although I'd survived a decade out here on my own with limited ventures in to the Collective, every trip to the Trade Path carried the risk of exposure. I fingered the card in my pocket, running the pad of my thumb along the curved edge ritualistically.

The two moons sat high, shining brilliantly through the tiny skylight above me. I stared up at them, begging for sleep to come, knowing I'd need all of my strength for the trip ahead. Methodically, I mentally listed everything in the pack, recounted my steps around the sled, visualized the satisfactory state of the reins for Tonk and Tilo. Everything was ready, so why couldn't I shake this feeling that something was missing?

***

My body ached and my joints were stiff. I had curled up in the most awkward position while I slept, and the pain throughout my body served as the ramification of my restlessness. The boys pawed the ground, restless and playful. Their excited energy flowed to me and eased the tension in my shoulders. I rolled my head and shook out my arms, watching as Tilo tackled Tonk and snow fluffed up into the air around them.

"Okay, boys, knock it off. Time to get on the move." I harnessed them both to the front of the sled and secured their protective booties to their paws. I triple checked the twine on the packs, and then planted my feet in the sled.

"Run," I hollered over the whistling winds. The boys started out with a steady drive through the snow-covered forest floor. Tall thin evergreens sagged heavily with a drapery of fluffy white flakes. Out of the corner of my eye, I watched the sun creep up in hues of pink and orange, the vibrant colors alluding to the warmth they'd once possessed. I pulled my hood in tighter around my face as the dogs picked up speed across the barren terrain.

Visibility was good and that meant we'd get to the Collective that much faster. I didn't want to spend any more time than necessary out in the open expanse of wilderness. I had a small set of arrows with me, but if we encountered any beasts like the one that paid us a visit the night before, they wouldn't be enough to protect us. Without my spear, we were vulnerable to the wildlife out here and as good as dead if they caught our scent on the icy air.

My forethought in packing served us well as Tonk and Tilo fought hard against the ever-increasing altitude. Light loads meant less food for the trip, but the ability to move swiftly up the mountain. If we could make it back down the other side before nightfall, we would be sure to be at the Collective by midday tomorrow. The trees became shorter and the needles more dense as the altitude became increasingly more challenging. The boys slowed, their lungs fighting for air in the thin atmosphere. I jumped off the sled and ran around to the front, helping to haul the load. We were maybe a hundred yards from the peak. I could see the summit in the distance.

"Heel," I called out to the boys. We needed a break. No matter how badly I wanted to make it to the Collective in a day's time, I couldn't risk their health. Finding a flat spot surrounded by some jagged rocks and under the cover of a large pine tree, I prepared bowls of water for them.

Cruel and fierce wind bit at the small sections of skin left exposed by the hood of my coat. Tonk and Tilo pranced in place, fighting to keep warm and prevent their feet from freezing. Their booties weren't enough and we needed to move along fast. The boys lapped up their water and I capped the thermal canteen after granting myself a sip. Just before I pulled up my facemask to continue on the trail, I heard a rustle. Beasts at this elevation were rare, even rarer than out on the plains, but not impossible. T and T growled, the hair on their backs standing on end. The little hairs on my neck followed suit. I whipped off my hat, not wanting my vision obstructed by the various flaps and ties.

The distinct sound of a human foot crunching over packed snow brought reality crashing down on me. Fear coursed through my veins and brought with it a chill that could have turned steam into blocks of ice in midair. The Reaper stepped out from between the trees, his beard long and unkempt, fingers dirty, eyes hungry for victory.

Not me, I thought resolutely. *I will not be part of his cull.*

He walked forward methodically, measuring each step against the likelihood that I would scurry and give him the thrill of a chase.

"Looks like your luck ran out. How long have you been off the grid? Five, six years?" He appraised my body slowly. "You should be proud. Lots to brag about in the camp."

"No time for chatting. I have business to attend to at the Trade Path. I'm sure you understand." I pivoted in place as the Reaper circled around me. So confident in his bounty, the smug smile on his face incited a riot of anger and hatred that balled in the pit of my stomach.

"Why don't you make this easy on yourself and come willingly? I'd hate to have to rough up a pretty little thing like you." He flexed his fist and licked his lips.

Bile threatened to spill into my mouth. His next step toward me sent my reflexes flying. In one fell swoop, I released the boys, grabbed an arrow off my back and shot it directly at him. He darted away but the tip lodged itself deep in the meaty part of his shoulder. Instead of pulling it out, he broke it off, leaving the shrapnel to keep the wound plugged. A smart move, but the boys and I were smarter. A small flick of my wrist, the command nearly imperceptible to the human eye, and they knew what to do.

The boys barked in unison. I heard the first crack above us echo through the valley. Fighting the smile that wanted to spread across my lips, I spoke to the boys, my sarcasm heavy.

"Oh, no, boys. Quiet. We wouldn't want to disturb any of that heavy snowbank up there."

Another crack, louder this time, echoed through the trees. His eyes narrowed into angry slits as realization of my plan dawned on him. *Game on.* He looked off in the direction of the looming avalanche, relieving me of his scrutiny momentarily, but enough for me to launch myself at him. The boys barked louder and with more force. His breath left him in a rush as the heel of my palm connected with his solar plexus. I spun to plant my foot into his gut, but his arms wrapped around my torso before I could find purchase. Stench of body odor and sour breath rolled over my face as he hooked his arms under mine and laced his fingers behind my head.

He chuckled, assuming victory, and I struggled a bit to make him think he'd won. The moment I felt his arms relax in the slightest, I knew he'd let his guard down.

Not today, Reaper. Not ever, Affinity.

I planted my left foot and swiped his legs from under him with my right, tossing him over my shoulder. His body hit the ground with an audible thud. I smiled at his wide eyes right before I jabbed my last arrow into his throat. He choked and gurgled on the ground before me. I turned away from the gruesome sight, unable to watch the last light of life evaporate from his eyes.

Tonk and Tilo continued to bark and snap, the sounds reverberating off the mountain wall and echoing through the valley below. I hurried to secure their harnesses in place. On my command, they yanked the sled forward, resuming our ascent. We drove higher and higher until the rumble was dangerously close. The ground beneath us trembled and the sickening sound of trees groaning and snapping under the weight of snow echoed around me. The wave of white crested into my line of sight and I immediately yanked the boys to the right. We pushed hard and fast along the side of the mountain, never stopping, never looking back. My legs burned and my lungs felt like they were being sliced to ribbons. I drove deep into the evergreens until the crystal ocean of snow went still and silent.

Braving a glance behind us, I surveyed the huge path of the avalanche–white, quiet, and pristine, the only thing that could hide the bloody trail of violence from the Affinity. Blood pounded in my ears and the boys panted, collapsing onto the icy earth beneath our feet. My legs were wobbly and my arms were uncoordinated, like loose strings on the frayed edge of an old sweater. I let myself sink to the ground next to Tonk and Tilo. They both moved against my body, keeping me warm while allowing us to absorb a moment of serenity. I kissed them both on their muzzles and stroked them in long, grateful pats.

Fresh flakes of snow drifted down from the skies, gently dusting my hair and the boys' fur. A new storm was headed our way and we couldn't camp at this high elevation overnight.

"Come," I commanded, first kneeling in the fresh powder, then hopping to my feet. Tilo and Tonk needed to see I still had the strength to lead. I was their master. If I needed them to go on, they must know I had the will to get us there. I peered up the mountain, squinting through the little flurries that surrounded me. We were still near the peak, but without a clear path to follow over it we would be traveling blind. The once trusted trail was buried now beneath thirty feet of snow.

We resumed our ascent with methodical steps and ambitious intentions. The will to survive was our only sustenance as we fought through the ice and snow. Our fortitude and fight to live another day led us through the maze of trees and the mysterious veil of snowflakes. We slowed from time to time but never stopped, our motivation to succeed outweighing the fatigue in our limbs and the hunger in our bellies.

The sunlight faded back to the familiar pinks and oranges that had greeted us at dawn, only now the tepid colors were a sign that the cold dark of night would be upon us soon. We crested the peak of the mountain only moments after the second moon had risen. A few hundred feet down the opposite side, Tonk, Tilo, and I sought shelter for the night in a hollowed out section of rock. I donned my thermal socks and hid the three of us under a heat-reflecting sheet. Prayers were silent on my lips as I begged the spirits to let us survive the night. The wind howled and I squeezed my eyes shut at the nagging sense of discontent that had settled in my stomach.

***

The peace of the morning light lent good humor to my mood as we prepared to make our way down. The fresh snow that had blanketed our surroundings through the night lay in a light cover over the jagged rocks and spiny-needled bushes. I unwound the knot I had tied myself into under the cover of darkness, stretching my arms high and pointing my toes. Relief spread through me knowing that our meager coverage had protected us until the morning light.

"Tonk. Tilo." I whistled low, the command designed to draw their attention at close range but not carry far or echo through the forest. We needed to arrive at the busiest time; more people meant more coverage. The boys made quick work of their small portions of food and we set out with anticipation tempered by trepidation.

I found our way back to the trail with a combination of my compass, some luck, and a lot of help from the boys. In the shadow of my narrow escape from the Reaper, my mind wandered back to life with my parents. Life before they were stolen from me and I was left to fend for myself.

My parents had told me stories of the promises that the Affinity made when it all began. Childhood history lessons were laced with bitter tones and encased in barely tempered rage. My mother often became emotional, sometimes filled with sorrow and other times bubbling with anger, when we read about the Green Age. At the time, I didn't understand how unstable political and economic circumstances were so enchanting. She'd tried to explain "freedom". I thought she was crazy.

As a kid, I didn't understand my parents' discontent with the Affinity. We had a good life, I thought. We were given enough to eat with our monthly rations, we had a warm house, and my mom and dad loved each other. They were my world. As I matured, I noticed an undercurrent of gratitude in their love that never faded. The affection they felt for each other colored all of their interactions. I often watched them chat about the day's plans while my mother cooked quinoa and cranberry porridge. My mother would touch my father's shoulder to accentuate a point, or my father would peck her on the cheek, thanking her for his breakfast.

They were appreciative of each other in a way that I didn't often witness between other couples in the Collective. They clung to each other as if one day they might be separated, or one day they might become lost. I asked my mother once, "Why do you worry so much when Dad goes to the farming house?" She replied, "One day you'll understand what it is to love someone with all of your heart. One day you'll fear losing that person, too." Years passed before I understood why she thought she might lose my dad.

Politics were a touchy subject as well. My father responded to news and current events with a generally dismissive air. My mother used to bring up new decrees, her cheeks reddening and her brow knotting as she filled my father in on the finer points of the newest rules and regulations, her pursed lips blowing the steam across her mug of tea. My father wouldn't discuss the laws or the politics surrounding them. He just shook his head and muttered words of disdain. He didn't read *The Affinity Herald* nor did he visit the Collective Room Meetings. He always shut off our transmitter before the daily Presidential Address.

One night, as I pretended to be asleep, I heard what I assumed to be a quarrel between my parents. I always slept with the door to my bedroom cracked open; the sound of my mother and father sharing, whispering, even giggling into the night was my version of a lullaby. That night the sounds were different, unnerving, as their voices became heated with anger and rose with intensity. The final words of the conversation carved their shape into my mind. Desperation rang clear in my mother's voice.

"They promised only for two generations, Stenor. Only two! It's been *twelve*. Now what? What's this mean for Cressie, for her future? What's this mean for us if they find out?"

Of course, when the Affinity did find them, they were sent to the work camps with all the other outlaws and deviants, forever separated from the one person they loved more than anything: their soulmate. The hollow look on my mother's face as the Reapers read their charges aloud remained the last memory I had of her. If I hadn't been of age, they would've sent me to a camp as well. Luckily, I fell in the buffer zone, as we call it: old enough to care for myself but still too young to be Matched. I often wondered who had it harder, my parents or myself. I suspected the former and not the latter.

I shoved the memories of my parents to the recesses of my mind, covering the sentimentality with dust-cloths of survival. The boys slowed their pace, the thicker section of forest signaling how close we were to the foothills. The sun brought with it unseasonal warmth. I dropped my hood and cherished the weak rays as they beat down on the crown of my head. I could hardly see the first moon in the nearly blue sky. Winter always had the lightest cloud cover, the high pressure of the atmosphere coupled with the distance from the sun driving away the puffy white menaces and allowing for the topaz sparkle above. Even though the cold hit deeper, most people fared better in winter than during the volatility of spring. I'd take white heavens over freezing rain and solar explosions any day.

We were forced to slow our pace. Trees, crowded and dense, surrounded the trail as it wound tightly down the heavily sloped section of mountain. Their branches sagged, heavy with snow and layers of ice packed one upon the next. Tonk and Tilo made every effort to step along the treacherous path before us with the light-footed expertise of a deer mouse. We had survived an avalanche only half a day ago. None of us were interested in reliving that excitement any time soon. I realized snow wasn't our enemy here though, as I surveyed the expanse of icicle-laden trees before us.

I had hoped the worst of our environmental threats would be the giant snarling beasts and our brush with being buried alive. I hadn't expected the unseasonably strong sun and thick, shining daggers of hanging ice. Some of them were as thick as the trunks of the trees where they hung, with spear-tipped points sharp enough to cut glass. The boys knew to tread lightly so as not to disturb the surroundings. I trailed behind, steering the sled, keeping it as far from the bases of the giant pines as possible.

I had never once considered we would face icicles on this trip. They belonged to spring, when the sun shone in irregular patterns and the snow tried its hand at being water, only to freeze on its way to the ground. They were tricky to avoid, some hanging low and forcing me to crouch down to pass under them. I looked up to assess my clearance on a particularly long icicle in my path, when I lost my footing and slid into the base of a skinny-limbed tree. Tinkling echoed like an eerie song of deadly wind chimes just before the sounds of breaking glass exploded around us. The air shimmered and light refracted off the flying shards of ice, blinding me with gleaming rainbows and sparkling like diamonds as a shower of icicles rained down around us. I did my best to take cover under my parka and hoped that T and T had jumped out of the way in time. The falling daggers drilled down into the ground around us. One pierced the arm of my parka, but the fur lining inside protected the delicate skin beneath.

"Boys, you okay?" They answered with short barks, alerting me to their location and their well-being. I found both dogs standing at the side of the sled, waiting at attention for my command. I walked to them, intending to praise their fast reflexes and offer rewards of dried meat and water. But when I leaned down to rub Tonk's head, I saw the growing smattering of red on the snow beneath him. Despite the cold wind whipping across my face, the lids of my eyes peeled back wide with alarm.

"Okay, Tonk, you've got to lie down on this." I spread out my tarp for him. The blood came out in constant rivulets from the gash behind his shoulder. I had only seconds to assess the extent of the wound before I risked him becoming too weakened to continue. I ran my hands along his fur until I found the slice in his skin. As far as icicle injuries went, Tonk had fared decently.

"Clean cut through the skin, no missing pieces, no damage to any muscles or bones," I told him. "You're going to be fine, but I've gotta move quick. Oh, Tonk," I took a deep breath, "I'm sorry to do this to you, but we're gonna have to stitch you up right here."

Tilo whimpered and laid down next to him. I retrieved my supplies from the sled, unfolded a clean needle from a scrap of cloth, and unraveled a length of thread. Kneeling down next to Tonk, I watched as the blood started to mat the fur around the wound, the freezing temperature causing it to congeal as it hit the air.

I pulled out a vial of numbing liquid, letting only a few drops fall onto the long narrow slice in his flesh. His breathing calmed and the tension in his body eased as the anesthetic deadened the exposed nerves in his flesh. Gritting my teeth in solidarity for his endurance, I went about the gruesome job of dousing the wound with antiseptic before sewing fine, even stitches in the dense weight of Tonk's coat. I worked as quickly as I could, knowing the numbing liquid would wear off soon and each stitch would be excruciating without it.

"You're doing good, boy, real good. There we go, last stitch." Tilo hadn't moved an inch. He never left his brother's side. I knew he would have taken every stitch for him if he could. I rubbed salve over the sutures and put a fresh few drops of numbing liquid on the wound.

"Stand for me, Tonk. Up." Tonk dragged himself to his feet. I sat in front of him, looking into his eyes, studying his face. His wore an expression of weary determination. I doled out water and meat rations to both of the boys, but Tilo dropped his portion at Tonk's feet.

"Good boy, Tilo. I love him too." I scratched his head and cuddled him for a minute. The love and support those dogs gave to each other often left me longing for a sibling. I appreciated their companionship and their trust, even if they weren't my flesh and blood. I might never have a bond with another person the way they did with each other, but they knew me and I knew them and that was enough.

We moved, slow and steady, the rest of the way down the mountain and through the foothills. Even though it meant we lost nearly another half day, I gave Tonk frequent stops to rest and let him have most of the remaining water in our canteen. When we were at the base of the foothills, I searched again for a hidden spot to camp for the night.

"What would we do without caves, huh?" I asked Tilo over my shoulder while setting up our shelter. "Boys, stay. I'm gonna make us a fire before the sun gets too low."

I collected wood in the surrounding brush while the boys recuperated under the thermal blanket back at camp. Under the cover of dusk, our small fire warmed our cold and tired bones while we shared a small feast of quinoa porridge.

"You guys deserve this. You've worked hard." I added in a mutter under my breath, "You deserve better, but it's all I've got."

I extinguished the fire as soon as the second moon shone bright in the sky. I administered another round of numbing drops to Tonk to get him through the night and piled branches and snow onto the sled to camouflage it from searching human eyes. Beasts were no longer a concern. They stayed away from the Collective. They might be big, but they were more than outnumbered. I was glad to be rid of them for the rest of our trip.

We were a full day behind now, and the end of the Trading Week meant our pickings most certainly would be slim. Foot traffic on the Path typically decreased as the week went on. The rations available would dwindle, leaving few trading options until the next month when rations were given out again. But fewer Traders also meant less of a cloak of anonymity, and I couldn't afford any more mishaps.

I snuggled with Tonk and asked him, "How much longer do you think we have?" He snorted in response, the warm air making tiny clouds puff out of his nostrils. I chuckled, imagining him as one of those big scaly dragons from my mother's bedtime stories, the kind that breathed fire and melted the ice tower, freeing the stolen princess.

"Forever? Yeah, you're right. We're too smart for them. They'll never catch us. Even if they find us, they'll never catch us."

I went to bed under the two moons that night dreaming of running, but not of being chased. I dreamt of my parents leading the way through a green and yellow field of grass while I followed. I dreamt of running and laughing, toward blue skies and freedom, with happiness in my heart and love in my hand.

CHAPTER TWO
A Fair Trade

People hurried around the Collective, their excitement casting out tendrils of buzzing energy that swirled around me. I had nearly forgotten about the holiday season. Festivities were in full swing. In this state of constant winter, the snow blanketing the low slanted roofs and frosting the glass in the windows had lost its sentimental charm.

The citizens of the Affinity worked hard to keep the festivities of the Green Age alive. Sprigs of shrubbery and thin branches of needled pine were woven into intricate wreaths, embellished with glossy red ribbons, and hung throughout the town. A colossal tree grew in the center of the Collective. It stood mighty and proud amid the flurry of people at its base. Silver and gold ornaments, each made by a different set of hands and symbolic of its family of origin, adorned the branches from top to bottom. The enticing warm glow of candles shone from shop windows, wasting the heat that could be found so readily here in this place of luxury. Large gilded bells hung from heavy-gauge wires strung from the center of the tree, exploding in a starburst pattern across the Collective. Despite the desperation with which they clung to the rituals, the magic of Christmases past had faded, buried under two hundred years of ice and snow.

I regarded the controlled chaos of the Trade Path. Too many vendors and too much clutter were punctuated by shouting people and boisterous laughter. In the relative peace of the center of town, the thick din of the Trade Path carried far. The noise served as a beacon, leading the way to the electric frenzy of commerce. I tied Tilo and Tonk to the free post among all of the other sled teams. Most of them were too old to actually work any longer. Their rotund bellies and fluffy coats spoke to their positions as house pets rather than pack members. Living in the plushy comfort of the Collective provided little opportunity to put their instincts to use. The dogs were still utilized to pull sleds to and from the Trade Path once a month, but dragging a few pounds of grain and a pile of cotton fabric was hardly enough of a challenge to work off the calorie-dense diets of their privileged circumstances. The lithe and rugged build of Tonk and Tilo looked sharper and more angular, a stark contrast to the rounded girth of those dogs.

I checked Tonk's wound, weighing his immediate need for comfort against his ability to make the trip home in this condition. He would need the few remaining drops to get back on the mountain tonight. I considered the fact that our pack would be lighter and we would get home faster. I could press a new vial as soon as we got there. I reached my hand out to place a drop on his wound, pulling it back momentarily.

"No," I shook my head at myself, "I know you need this. Here, boy, relax." I let one drop slip from the vial, shimmering as it hit the rough stitches and dissipated across the slice in his flesh. Regret slithered around in my insides. I should never have let my supplies run so low. I watched with a pang of guilt as they settled in under the shelter of the hitching post. I emptied the canteen for them, knowing I could refill it from the reservoir in the Path, and tossed them some more dried rind.

The overcrowded Trade Path provided perfect cover for an Outlier like me. So many faces, all blending and mixing with each other until you're swimming in a blur of human features. I held my satchel close, filled with the rare herbs that so few in the Collective were knowledgeable enough to grow on their own. The Affinity had stopped growing medicinal herbs a hundred years ago on the premise that their modern pharmaceutical facilities produced concoctions superior to anything naturally occurring. The industrial building that once served as a hydroponic greenhouse for all of the medicinal herbs had been stripped of its contents and replanted with more grain and legumes to meet the continually increasing demand for rations.

Some citizens were avid traders, bringing their surplus rations to the same spot every month, while others, usually the older citizens, had a tendency to hoard their extra rations, the fear of going without deeply ingrained. Those who worked in the fruit and vegetable facilities were the most frequent traders, given the short shelf life of their products. On the other hand, the grain and legume harvesters came to the Trade Path least often. Those with cloth, silicates, metals, and pharmaceuticals came intermittently, mostly depending on their own wants or needs.

I knew the history of the Trade Path well, and how it became a necessity after the Affinity had taken over and begun a system of production, allotment, and disbursement of rations. My father's family had passed down a journal belonging to an ancestor who had lived through the rise of the Affinity. The handwritten entries were full of details about the struggles both his family and the new government had faced in the wake of an Ice Age. Frozen ground meant no more farming. Animals of all types became extinct, and raising animals for consumption had ended a century earlier in hopes of preventing the inevitable change in climate. The majority of people had starved to death. Those who remained passed down their memories of acute fear and pain to the generations that followed. Confronted with a society so fearful of going without that they continued to hoard their rations, exacerbating their malnourishment, their habits threatened to derail the entire platform of the new government: to propagate the growth of the human race.

After two generations of the Affinity's rule, muddled by consistently declining birth rates and increasing death rates, the human race neared extinction. The Affinity needed to force the citizens to interact as well as utilize their rations. Vibrant three-dimensional images of propaganda viewed on my holo-tab remained lodged in the corners of my mind. Their presence in my history lessons were like horrific omens of the future we now inhabited. Like all good power-hungry governments, the Affinity made huge strides toward total ownership of its citizens. As people became more comfortable with the availability of food, the Trade Path flourished. Complacency enveloped their entitled lives. Though the death rate declined, the birth rates were still lagging. The evolution of the totalitarian government, who controlled our very sustenance, who maintained the flow of food, energy, and medicine, had carved a clear path for the Matching Laws. The last vestiges of autonomy were swiftly stripped from life under the Affinity's rule.

Growing up with parents who were part of the network of Outliers, these facts were considered atrocities, meant to rouse the rebels and speak to the instincts for independence and freedom. Yet there I sat, ready to infiltrate their ranks for what I couldn't cultivate on my own. The ironic nature of my position was not lost to me.

I had trustworthy relationships with a few citizens that were usually interested in my tea leaves, and one older man, Graham, who relied on my balsam fir resin to treat his arthritis. I would save his visit for last. Visiting with Graham filled me with a sense of familial legacy, even if we weren't blood kin.

He knew of my Outlier status, though I didn't speak of my circumstances and he never asked. The topography of Graham's face, with deep valleys of experience and high ridges of wisdom, conveyed an understanding that needed no words. I felt an envy lurking behind his bored expression, that he hadn't chosen the same path a lifetime ago.

During our last exchange, he'd spoken with the bitterness of bile on his tongue. "I'm not taking that poison they make. Who knows what's really in it?" He'd leaned close, his eyes locked on mine with a strength that contradicted his wrinkled face and wispy white hair, and added, "They already took all of my pleasure. I won't let them have my pain, too."

I skirted around the smaller groups of Traders, heading for the roiling mass of bodies that churned and bubbled with the manufactured mirth of the season. Silk and legumes were in high demand, but silicates and metals, which I needed for building my solar panel, were mostly ignored. This would prove to be in my favor. With the impending holiday meals to prepare, citizens were all clamoring for the best food and anything suitable for gifting. I slid through a throng of citizens fighting for the last cluster of grapes and headed for the grain traders. I knew I could easily have the highly sought after fruit with such a valuable trade as my fur pelt, but I knew better than to draw attention to myself.

I smiled when I found Servelle in her usual spot along the edge of the row. Her face brightened as I plopped my satchel on her table. She bounced a cherubic infant on her lap, though it continued to wail and hiccup in discomfort. I worked to hide a grimace at the piercing sound of the infant's cries. It seemed we would both benefit well from today's trade.

"Hi, Servelle, whatcha have for me today? Boy, she's got a set of lungs on her." The eerie sensation of being watched prickled over my skin. I spotted a young man surveying our transaction closely. He was thin, too thin to be a citizen. He had to be new to the lifestyle. Probably looking for clues as to how an Outlier could infiltrate the Trade Path and not get caught. I did my best to be a good example for him as I worked my trade.

"Oh, Cressenda, she's just miserable. She's been crying like this for days. Please tell me you have peppermint today? I have lots of beans for you." Servelle tried to cover her desperate pleas with a lilt of hope.

"I've got it, and some lemon balm tea for you, too. It will help calm your nerves. I'm sure you're rattled from all that crying. Has Hart been working at the mill?"

"Yes, his foot healed well once we got that medicinal pack from you. I never would've thought we could soak some dried plants and cure his swelling, but you were right, it worked like magic."

"Shhh, Servelle, don't say that so loud." We laughed together at false secrecy and finished our business with more pleasantries. I walked away with beans as well as some grain, which would suit the boys and me well for a couple of months.

I zeroed in on the part of the Path further down, where the minerals and metals were traded. I had carefully sectioned my fur into four pelts: one to trade for silicone, one to trade for aluminum, another for a spool of copper wire, and last but most important, one for salt. I had to add a new solar panel to power the second, larger hydro-planter I'd built, but without the salt our meat would spoil or burn if it stayed buried in the snow for too long.

The Outlier boy followed closely, inching nearer as I haggled with the silicone trader, who wore the pristine white clothing common to those who worked in cleanrooms.

Those types never really let go of the sterility of their work environment.

"I want that one." He crossed his skinny arms over his concave chest. I quirked my head as I considered the power he must have felt here in the Path and how it contrasted against the daily impotence of his existence.

"Not happening. But this one is prettier. Think how much your wife will love fashioning a stole to wear at the festivities." I had him and I knew it. I waited in silence and smiled with victory when his shoulders slumped.

"You're right." He shook his head and took the pelt from my hands with resigned defeat. Another trader nearby caught an eyeful of my bargaining chip and was more than willing to give up his entire aluminum ration along with half a spool of copper for two of my pelts.

High on my success, I danced along toward Graham and his table of trinkets. The Path overflowed with citizens desperate to trade on the last day of the trading week. They needed to gather everything for their holiday celebrations before the second moon rose that night. I had brought a square of balsam resin especially for Graham, along with a few other sundry herbs in my satchel, just in case I came across something unexpected.

My body jostled, confusion marring my thoughts as someone bumped against me. The force sent me spinning as my satchel was violently yanked off my arm. I righted myself and caught sight of the back of the young Outlier's form as he shoved his way through the crowd.

Fear made him fast, but anger and adrenaline gave me speed and accuracy. As much as I didn't want to draw unnecessary attention to myself, I would not let him out of the Path with my property. A large group of busybodies had circled around a trade that had de-escalated into shouts and disparaging remarks. Weaving myself through the holes and knots of people, frustrated "excuse me" and "sorry" pushed out of my mouth as feeble tools to widen my path. Frustration mounted as I watched the boy gain distance from me. Impulsively, I yelled out, "Stop him!"

Panic stopped me cold. Maybe no one heard me. Surely I couldn't have drawn attention to myself over the excitement of a trade gone bad. Much to my dismay, two large Guards stepped out from the shadows and into the Path. One grabbed the Outlier boy, roughly pulling my satchel from him before pinning his arms behind his back.

Serves him right, I thought. That kind of behavior gave Outliers a bad name. We didn't steal, and we certainly didn't kill other people to get what we needed, even if that was what the Affinity wrote on official sentencing documents. True Outliers lived by a code—a code that this kid clearly hadn't been informed of or didn't care to respect.

The second Guard stepped into view, pointing over to my satchel.

"That belongs to you, I assume?"

The boy glared at me as if I was the source of our now very delicate problem.

"Yeah, uh, yes, it's mine."

I looked up at the Guard's face, working hard to retain my composure. His serious and authoritative expression wasn't stern enough to distract from his handsome features. He took his time, surveying me from head to toe. Striking blue eyes shone out from his dark features, the kind of blue that was accented by brilliant white patterns in the iris. Pretty as he was, I wouldn't go down without a fight. I felt around in my pocket, palming the rough handle of my knife. The least effective of my weapons, but all I had left at this point.

"He took this from you?"

Anger coursed through my veins. The kid couldn't get out of this now. A twinge of guilt flexed in my heart as I answered, "Yes."

"Young man, I will need your key card." The boy shook his head. His fate was sealed at that moment. "No key card? Roth, this boy is an Outlier. Take him to the Council."

The kid struggled initially, but soon slumped in defeat as the Guard dragged him though the now clear Trade Path. A long column of onlookers lined the street, gawking at the boy who would surely be the highlight of tonight's Address.

"Miss, may I run your key card, please, so that we can log your complaint against the Outlier?"

Damn. I should have let the kid have my bag. I could have easily made a new one out of some hemp cloth back at my cabin. Now I faced a crossroads. Did I run, hoping to disappear under the cover of the forest, or did I risk it and give him the electronic tracking device that would surely alert him to my subversive lifestyle? I had been off the grid for a good ten years. The status that would appear when he ran my card would be the end, of either him or me, depending on how fast I could run. I gave the Path a once-over, surmised that my odds of escape were nil, handed my card over and waited for the inevitable showdown.

***

Everything moved in slow motion, my heart screaming in my chest, begging me to flee. The "fight" side of my fight-or-flight instinct didn't surrender at the sight of the Guard's broad shoulders and towering height. He stood a good foot taller than me, with coal-colored locks poking out in an unruly fashion from his grey woven cap. The light grey and white fitted uniform, standard issue of the Affinity Government Guard, only served to accentuate his dominating presence. But I wouldn't submit to his power. I'd resist out of sheer will to survive.

He held the reader in his hand with purpose, focused on his security duties, so formal in his stance. I watched the red light blink, blink, blink while it read the complicated pattern of dots and squares that encrypted every piece of information about my life, from my hair color to my origin of birth to the whereabouts of my parents.

I knew the moment that he saw my status as a "Missing Person". None of us were actually missing. Each and every Outlier had left of their own accord. Citizens weren't abducted, coerced, or tricked into leaving the Collective. Rarely, someone was born an Outlier, but births in the wild were few and far between. Most citizens left because they didn't want to ever be Matched, or had been Matched to someone they truly feared marrying. Sometimes young couples ran off together to avoid being Matched to another. Not often, though. And those kids usually returned to the Collective when they learned the true hardships of surviving on their own.

When the words flashed on his screen, his brow bunched and his nostrils flared. I took one small step to the left, still considering trying to escape. The Guard reached out and grabbed me, his strong arm holding me in place. One large boot-clad foot was planted on the outside of my legs as he brought his body as close as he could without actually pressing against me.

"Is it true?" he whispered to me while searching my face for any sign of denial. A forlorn sadness crossed his face before the mask of authority set in place again.

"Just do what you have to, Breeder, and get it over with," I spat at him through gritted teeth and a clenched jaw.

He stepped back, his hand still wrapped tight around my arm, and drew in a deep breath. The warm air billowed out of his lips when he spoke. "Sorry, miss, I believe my reader is malfunctioning."

Confused and irritated by the way he was dragging out the scene, I tried to yank my arm from his grasp, but he didn't budge. Did he get some sick satisfaction out of messing with my head? I knew what was waiting for me at the opening of the Trade Path: ten armed Guards and an electrified invisible cage that would encase me as I was marched to the Council. Outliers were treated as if they were some kind of violent threat to society. Our only offense: we wanted the freedom to reproduce with whomever we chose, or not at all. We didn't threaten anyone's life but our own. If only the Affinity saw it that way.

The Guard's hold was unrelenting. Anger melted into fear. Adrenaline chilled my blood, ceasing the roiling boil of hate that bubbled though my veins. I realized this man could take me, could hurt me, and no one would be any the wiser. The world already considered me "disappeared". There wouldn't be any search parties, and my name wouldn't appear on the screen during the weekly Affinity Address when they listed those who had gone missing. The days of people looking for me were long gone. There'd be no evidence that I had been here. I held my knife tighter, refusing to be completely at his mercy.

"Why are you...? I mean...it doesn't matter." Conflict apparently raged in his brain, pulling the lines of his face taut. However, what plagued his conscience was completely lost to me. He led me, still with his vice-like grip on my arm, to a spot between vendors, out of the way of the traders' prying eyes. "You should go. They will come looking for you if I don't take you out there soon. I'll get your bag back to you. Look for me here next trading session, and I'll return it to you. Now go. Quickly."

I didn't move a muscle. For one, he still held my arm with the desperation of a man clinging to the memory of a lost love; but more than that, this mythical being in front of me had me paralyzed.

"You...you're a...sympathizer." It sounded dirty as the words passed between my lips. I wanted to snatch them back and swallow them down again. The sting of my insult was evident in the painful expression that settled on his face.

"It doesn't matter what I am. You want to be free, don't you? Then go." His authoritative facade crumbled and the innocent hurt of a young boy dripped from his soul as he spoke. "You won't get far enough if you don't get out now."

I placed my hand over his, unlatching his fingers one at a time from the tender inside of my bicep. My steps were measured and controlled as I backed away from the Guard. I neared the clear walkway of the Trade Path just as a shrill alarm sounded. Every transaction halted and everyone held their breath for a split second, merchants and traders alike. In the blink of an eye, the entire population of the Path turned to the entrance and moved hurriedly, as if they were trying to contain a generalized franticness.

"What is it? Where are they going?" I asked no one in particular.

"It's a blizzard warning."

I cursed. A blizzard. I'd never make it home now. Conditions would be impossible: no visibility, forty-foot snowdrifts, and gale-force winds. The boys and I would never survive. I stood, motionless, while bodies spun and twirled on the periphery of my consciousness. I was stuck in the Collective with nowhere to go and, worse, nowhere to hide.

"Come with me," the masculine timbre commanded over my shoulder before lacing his fingers in mine. His gentle hold of my hand gave me comfort and lulled me into a hypnotic state. The Guard led me forward until I broke from my daze.

"Let me go!" I yanked my hand from his. "I have to get out of here. I have to beat the blizzard."

Before I could break into a sprint, the Guard whirled me around. I teetered, stunned by the force. He moved in close and arched over me while he spoke. Not to intimidate but to cover me, protecting me from the eyes around us.

"You'll never make it. Never. Come with me. You can wait out the storm at my cabin. When it's over, you'll be free to go." His eyes searched my person for the answer to the question in his mind. *Wherever it is you live.*

I stared at him, doubtful and distrusting. I had only seconds to decide if this tall, hulking citizen of the Collective, official of the Affinity, could really, truly be a sympathizer.

"You can trust me," he promised in earnest. I wanted to believe him, if only so that I didn't face a frozen, icy death out on the top of the mountain.

"Let's go," I whispered, trying to feel as confident in my decision as my voice sounded.

CHAPTER THREE
The Arrival

My feet hit hard on the pavement of the nearly empty Trade Path until we spilled out to the hitching post along with the other stragglers. A whirlwind of bodies moved through the center of town. Frenzied citizens clamped down sled lockers and yelled at their overweight dogs to pull faster, harder, careening across iced-over sled paths as they scurried toward the safety of their cabins.

Tonk and Tilo paced, the frenzied humans surrounding them causing nervous anxiety to coil in their muscles. They knew we needed to run, to get out, not just from the craziness in our midst but the telltale increased air pressure. Surely the boys had felt the blizzard coming well before that alarm sounded. If I hadn't been distracted by Tonk's injury, I would have too.

Struggling to get my bearings amid all the commotion, my mind felt as chaotic as the scene before me. My insides grew wobbly with confusion. Was this plan safe or just insane? My hands shook as I worked to untie the boys' harness from the post. The Guard had disappeared and I considered making a run for it. The decision was made for me when he came flying into the hitching post on a sleek solar-powered snowmobile.

"Follow me. It's a straight shot through to the edge of the Collective. I'll go slow."

Finally, I freed the boys and jumped onto the sled. We wasted no time cutting through the center of the tiny town at the base of the mountain. Collectives operated as if they were the same as the big cities of the Green Age, but in actuality they were small and close-knit, consisting of a few thousand families at best. My sled sped along the trail carved by the Guard's mobile. The white flurries came down faster and faster, the distance between us growing despite my exhaustive efforts to keep up. I yelled to Tonk and Tilo to pull harder. For this plan to work I would need to be strong and do it right. The frightening prospect of being at his mercy thrust my self-preservation instincts to the forefront of my actions. I'd go toe-to-toe with that behemoth of a man over my very survival if it came to that.

I knew Tonk was suffering; the wound in his side had to be tearing open at this breakneck pace. I prayed that he would make it to the shelter of the cabin.

"There. It's there, boys. GO!" I could see the grey smoke from the chimney just ahead. The Guard slowed his mobile and we gained ground. Tonk pushed hard through his pain with the promise of relief just off in the distance.

The windows of the Guard's house were crystal clear, providing a glimpse of the warm yellow light waiting inside. A small garage off to the side of the cabin gave shelter to his solar mobile and my sled. We stood at the access door in silence, both in disbelief that we were really going through with this dangerous endeavor.

"I'm Beckett. You should, um, you should know that."

"Cressenda...but you already knew that, I guess," I said, acknowledging he already knew everything about me from his handy little card reader. I stared at him, examining his face for a trace of malice, anything subversive or alarming, but all I found was a strong jaw grinding on itself and a deep crease of worry through his forehead.

"Yeah, I remember." He smiled at the useless formality.

I laughed, not just at my awkward introduction but the absurdity of the whole situation. Beckett used his key card to open the access door to his humble-sized cabin. When I hesitated, he looked at me inquisitively, searching for an answer to my reluctance.

"The boys...can they come in? I won't leave them out in the blizzard. I'd rather die on the mountain with them." I was adamant.

"Yes, yes. I wouldn't make them stay outside through this. Now get in here." He ushered us through the access and hurriedly closed it, flashing his card in front of an infrared reader on the wall beside us.

His home coupled an inviting mixture of Green Age styling with standard Collective accoutrements. Clean, smooth furnishings sat on top of wood flooring, the touches of old-world style giving it a cozy feeling. A small table with two chairs sat flush against a low wall separating the kitchen from the rest of the cabin. The kitchen itself consisted of only the necessary appliances. A large bed sat unobtrusively in the corner, leaving room for the centerpiece of the small living space: a plush upholstered sofa that faced a wide-mouthed wood-burning hearth. Between the sofa and the hearth, a large fur rug covered the expanse of wood, and I laughed heartily at the useless piece of decor, knowing full well that every house in the Collective had ambient-heating floors.

With a light laugh in his voice, he addressed my mirth. "Hey, it's a family heirloom." The boys had no qualms about the ridiculous rug and immediately took up residence in front of the hearth, warming their paws and melting the remaining flakes of snow that clung to their coats. I stood just a few steps in from the door, my muscles coiled tight and my senses on high alert. Distrust ran deep in my veins, and a cozy fur rug next to a warm fire couldn't erase the threat encased in this cabin.

"You can come in, you know. Hang your coat over there and I'll bring you a cup of tea." Beckett pointed to the set of hooks on the wall next to the access door and then waved me over to the sofa. His immense size contrasted so comically against the short counters and low cabinets of his kitchen. He dwarfed the electric kettle in his massive palm. Shrugging off my coast and stepping out of my boots, I watched as he pulled out two mugs from the cabinet. Their size was miniaturized like children's playhouse furnishings as he held their handles with one long finger.

Perched on the edge of his sofa, I searched for signs of his personal life. I found nothing; no stray hairpins or flower-filled vases, no pictures on the wall, and no second pair of shoes next to the door. I felt around in my coat for my knife once more. What kind of man lived alone in the Collective? Was this a good thing?

Or would this man, this anomaly of the Affinity, be my captor in the end?

"Thank you," I said with an edge of irritation as I reached for the steaming mug of tea. The muted green color of the ceramic cup reminded me of the fir trees that lined the edge of the Collective. Beckett's house sat on the furthest rim of town, nestled right up against the thick forest of balsam and pine.

"Balsam!" I exclaimed and jumped down to where the boys were resting on the floor. "Damn it. I forgot to get more resin." I crawled over to Tonk and laid my hand on his ribs. His heart pounded and he panted hard as he fought through the pain, the warrior in him too proud to whimper as I inspected the wound. The stitches held, but the gash was raw and inflamed.

"It's okay, boy, it's okay." I smoothed his coat in an attempt to provide some form of relief. "I have to go out there. You don't have to go with me, but I need to get some bark off those trees behind your cabin right now."

"Why do you need bark? What trees? Are you crazy?" Beckett hunched forward, his forehead scrunched in utter confusion. I shoved my feet back into my boots, leaving the laces trailing behind me. They made scraping noises against the floor as I stomped to get my coat.

"For pain relief." I explained while I pulled on my coat. "I cook the resin with vinegar, a few drops and the pain is gone for a couple of hours. He needs it. He needs it now. The pain must be unbearable. Tonk..." I choked on his name. My gaze shifted over to Tonk lying on the fluffy white rug, his chest rising and falling with the same rapid pounding of my guilt. I cursed myself. I cursed the blizzard. I cursed the entire situation. I wouldn't let Tonk suffer. I would not let him die in the house of this man I didn't know. Balsam had to be found, and it had to be found immediately.

"That's amazing. You can do that?" His wonderment would have been endearing if I wasn't panicked about Tonk's current state and the worsening storm outside.

"Yeah, but the last few drops I had were in my satchel. I have to get bark and press the resin." I stood in front of the access door tapping my foot. "Could you open this damn door so I can go out there? Um, I mean, *please*."

"You don't need to do that. Come here. I have a whole medic kit." The Guard took my hand and led me over to the table in his kitchen. The shock of his warm hand in mine dulled the buzz of anxiety bouncing around in my body. "Wait here."

Medic kits—a convenience of the Collective. I'd forgotten everyone had a supply of medicines and bandages readily available to treat most common aches and ailments.

Beckett handed me a large box with a hinged lid. Inside, a multitude of tiny vials and tubes were arranged alphabetically. Sterile cloth bandages of various sizes lay in a neat pile in the lower section alongside tape, scissors, tweezers, and a few other tools.

"Can I use anything I need?" I tried hard not to sound desperate but I felt like falling at his feet and begging for free rein of the cornucopia in front of me.

He nodded, bemused by my astonishment at what he regarded as a common household convenience.

"Which one is for pain, and which one heals?" I helped myself to a handful of the sterile cloths, tape, and the scissors.

"Here. This will do both, but use this to clean it." He placed one tube of ointment and a bottle of solution in my hand and nodded.

I took care to cut the fur around Tonk's wound down as close as I could to his skin. Using one cloth, I dabbed along the oozing cut. I reminded myself not to hurry, so frantic was I to help my beloved pack member. Once clean, I spread the ointment along the crudely stitched wound with another pad and taped the remaining pads to the closely cropped sections of fur surrounding it.

Tonk's relief was palpable. I released a huge sigh and snuggled against his chest, careful to keep my weight off his body. His heart had slowed to a normal pace and his breaths turned long and deep.

"That's it. That's my boy. You're such a soldier. Just rest now."

Lost in the elation of Tonk's remedied state, I started at the sound of Beckett's voice. The realization of my whereabouts slammed back into my head and my heart stalled.

"You really love those dogs, don't you?"

"They're all I've got. They're my family. I don't know what I'd do if I lost them." I rose from the floor and made stunted, awkward movements trying to decide where to sit.

"Go ahead, sit on the sofa. It's closer to your dogs." Satisfied with Tonk's heavy slumber, I curled myself into a ball on the sofa. Without the distraction of a medical emergency, the uncomfortable strangeness of my situation returned. I watched Beckett cross back to the sofa with a newly filled steaming green mug. A hint of déjà vu sprinkled in the air; we had just done this, not ten minutes earlier, but now everything seemed different.

He didn't sit with me. Rather, he went back and leaned against the low counter in the kitchen area. I didn't know who between the two of us wanted the space more. I supposed he wrestled with the same questions of our precarious circumstance that I did. What were we thinking, taking a risk like this? What would the consequences be if we were caught? Could we trust each other? And what did it mean if we couldn't?

I sipped my tea and stared at him. He stared at the fire. The longer I stared at him, the more intently he watched the long tongues of flame lick at the air.

"Do you regret it?" His head jerked up at the blatant nature of my question. "Do you regret helping me? I know you're risking a lot by doing this. I can still go, you know. I'm good at making it on my own out there."

His face hardened and he spoke with a curt assuredness. "I don't regret it."

Well, that wasn't much to go on. So he didn't regret it, but could I trust him to let me go? Or would this become some complicated ruse to get me to turn myself in? It didn't seem like it, but stranger things had happened. His face told little of his emotions, and those that he did reveal were innately masculine but far from telling. Considering the enormity of his risk in this situation, I did the only thing I could to ease my nerves and repay his supposed generosity.

"If you're hungry, I can cook." I moved into the kitchen and rummaged through his refrigerator. He didn't answer. He only watched me as I took over his kitchen, pulling out pans and searching through drawers.

Everything in the cupboard had been arranged in neat rows, all of his rations organized and accounted for. After a little deliberation on my part, I decided on a spicy dish to warm the uncomfortable chill between us. Lentils, beans, and dried chilies simmered on the electric range while I stirred, willing myself to conjure up a plan in case his kindheartedness was just a facade. It had been so long since I used a range top that the dish took longer than usual to heat through. There were dials and digital read-outs to complicate what was simplistic and rudimentary back at my cabin. Back at home I only had a filament coil attached to the power supply. I turned it "on" or "off". But here I could adjust the temperature to the tenth of a degree, control the direction of the circulation of heat through the coils, and set it to automatically turn off when the food reached a specific temperature. Very fancy. Unnecessary, but fancy. Of course, that was the way of the

Affinity and all the Collective. They had a knack for complicating the simple.

We were silent for a long time. I concentrated on the food while he pretended not to watch me. When the beans were tender and the lentils had softened to something edible, I plated everything and then stared at the dishes in front of me.

I absorbed the absurdity of what I had done. Who goes to the home of a Guard of the Affinity and cooks him dinner? A fool who wants to get arrested and live the rest of their days in a work camp, that's who. Did I really think he would let me go? I laughed at the shameful naive behavior that had led me here. Any Outlier worth their weight in salt knew never to trust the Affinity. Yet there I was, making spiced chutney for a Guard.

"What's so funny?" They were the first words he had spoken in nearly half an hour. I raised my eyebrows, vacillating between blowing off the question and letting the honesty pour out of my mouth. I went with the latter.

"Me. Here. That's what's funny."

"Yeah, it is kind of weird for you, I'm sure."

"You can say that again." My face gave away what I had tried to hide with my words.

"You're scared I'm not going to let you go, aren't you?"

"Well, I can't imagine why you would. It's your job to serve the Affinity." I set the plates at his two-person table against the short wall meant to demarcate where the kitchen ended and the dining area began.

"You don't know me, so you don't understand. I'm not going to turn you in. You can trust me."

He pushed the food around on his plate, inspecting the concoction before spearing a single bean with his fork. He smiled with surprise and then shoveled forkful after forkful into his mouth. He didn't take a break to breathe, let alone continue our conversation. I refilled his tea mug and took the seat across from him. I ate my food with less fervor but just as much enthusiasm. I hadn't had chilies since my plant died and I relished the delicious burn on my tongue. Spices were a rare trade. They weren't given as part of the rations, and only a few citizens were adept enough in hydro-horticulture to grow the plants themselves. I found it intriguing that Beckett had any at all. I'd lost my chili plant when the filament on one of my planters gave out on my last trip to the Trade Path. I hadn't been able to repair it without copper wire. Today's trip to the Path bought me the copper wire, but the likelihood that I would make it home to repair the planter remained questionable.

"That was so good. How do you know how to cook like that?" Beckett wiped at his mouth.

"I'm an Outlier, not a savage. I don't live that differently from you, ya know."

He pursed his lips and knotted his brow again. Clearly, Beckett didn't understand much about Outlier life. Every time I revealed another facet of my lifestyle, he reacted with more confusion. What kind of fallacies about Outliers floated around the Affinity these days?

I wanted to ease his confusion, so I volunteered more about my cooking skills. "My mother taught me how to grow the plants, and my father loved to cook."

His eyes popped open at mention of my family. Outliers weren't usually born in the wild. Most escaped the confines of life in the Collective, plunging their families into despair as the absence of their corpses added them to the Disappeared list. Even if they were captured, they were often already disowned by their families. They didn't speak of their families and their families didn't speak of them.

"I'm not an orphan, not like you think, anyway. My parents weren't Outliers. They were training me to be one, though. They helped a lot of people escape the Collective."

"They ran the underground?" His question was part shock and part awe.

"Yeah, well, no. They were part of it. People didn't stay at our house, my parents just helped coordinate where they would go. Sometimes they taught survival skills. Mostly they were involved in politics. It's what got them in trouble."

"How old were you when they were caught?"

"Sixteen."

"Did you stay in the Collective long?" He searched my face. "I don't recognize you."

"I left as soon as I could. The longer I stayed the more I risked being Matched." I shivered at the thought.

"Is that what you're afraid of?"

I tamped down my anger. I shouldn't have expected a citizen—more, a *Guard*—to understand the bondage inherent in being

Matched. They thought it was all well and good. Citizens were blind to the fact that they were nothing more than guinea pigs in a dirty science experiment.

"I'm not afraid of anything." I wished I could pin him to the back wall with the anger of my stare. He stared back, unflinching. Silence settled back in place of our sharing. The euphoria of the adrenaline brought on by the piquant dried chilies and the thrill of our adventure had worn off. We were left with nothing but the valley of distance between our mindsets.

Not one for staring contests, I stood and moved to clean up our dinner plates. I heard his chair scrape against the floor but didn't lift my eyes to see where he went. I was startled by the feel of his hand on top of mine.

"You're not my maid, you're my guest." He took the plates from me and dropped them into the sink.

CHAPTER FOUR
Speaking Truths

I stood, dumbfounded. His continued display of hospitality both confused and comforted me. No one had taken care of me in a very long time. A decade without another person to eat with, to clean up after, or even to argue with, left me dangling in uncertainty. Not only were Beckett and I diametrically opposed to each other's way of life, but he was also impossible to understand. Beckett with his broody face and hidden opinions. He had no qualms about asking me questions but, I realized, had volunteered very little about himself. When he sat on the sofa, I invited myself to join him, sitting as far from him as possible.

"You're not Matched? I mean, it's just you here, I can tell."

"No, it's just me. I'm not Matched."

"How?" I didn't need to elaborate; he knew what I was asking. No citizen of the Affinity made it past the age of twenty-one without being Matched.

"I was Matched, when I was younger, but Marielle, my wife, died in childbirth."

The silence clung to my neck and my arms, heavy with the burden of sadness. The information already shared between us was deep and fraught with dangerous emotion.

"I'm sorry. That's terrible. They haven't Matched you again?"

"I don't want to be Matched again."

"You loved her." Sorrow filled my heart, thinking that he had been a lucky one. He had loved his Match the way my parents had loved each other. "Did you know her before you were Matched?"

"No."

"Oh, then you were very lucky."

"No. I didn't love her."

I stared at him, stunned, though he didn't meet my gaze. I wanted to ask a million questions, and I almost did, but I sucked my lips between my teeth before the words came tumbling out. Much to my surprise, anger boiled to the surface of his skin and he spat out his story with venom on his tongue.

"We were considered a perfect Match. Our genes were supposed to create the healthiest, strongest offspring." The sound of the word "offspring" made me cringe. The Affinity had a way of taking the humanity out of everything, even the birth of our own children.

"What happened, if you don't mind me asking?"

"The baby was struggling. Her body wasn't supporting it anymore. She went into early labor. They tried to stop labor, and when those drugs failed, they tried to deliver the baby. She died on the operating table and our daughter died three hours later. So much for their superior methods."

Beckett was an unending string of contradictions and unexplained complexities. I wanted so desperately to know why he wasn't Matched after his wife had died, especially given his concise statement that he hadn't loved her. *None of my business*, I told myself. *Not my concern.* "I'm sorry you went through all of that loss. You must be pretty pissed off they got it wrong."

He looked at me like he wanted to kill me, or them, or everyone.

"They didn't get it wrong. Genetics are genetics, but there isn't anything they can do to circumvent Fate."

"Is that why you brought me here? Is this some attempt at rebellion?" I scoffed at the idea that harboring an Outlier was some kind of middle finger to the powers that be.

"I don't *attempt* things, I *do* them." Beckett set down his mug on the table at the end of the sofa. *What the hell kind of answer was that?* He stood and walked with deliberate steps to the edge of the hearth. The wide mouth of the stone enclave shrank when adjacent to his massive form. He tapped his fingers on the mantel, an interesting and ornate piece of antiquity. Many homes in the Collective had a wood-burning hearth, but few people chose to decorate their cabins with Green Age stylings.

"I like these pillows. Did she pick them, your wife? Your whole cabin is very cozy." He didn't answer, so I tried again. "Do you miss her?"

My prying question caught his attention. He surprised me, turning around to share a smile with me. His shoulders loosened and he nodded as he sat down again, this time closer to me.

"I do miss her. She was a good person, and she died far too young." He sighed and continued. "She didn't decorate, though. This is all my stuff."

"Pretty interesting choices." We laughed together. "It isn't exactly common for a guy to choose fluffy pillows and antique furnishings for a living room. Don't get me wrong, I love it all. I don't feel like I'm in a Collective cabin at all. It's just...unusual."

"Cressenda, we're not all the same, ya know. I'm my own person. We all are. Just because we don't run away doesn't mean we're mindless drones."

I crossed my arms over my chest and narrowed my eyes at him. That was exactly what citizens were, in my book. How could anyone live without his or her freedom? Being completely dictated to by some agency that professed to know what was better for you than you did for yourself? Beckett. He wasn't just a citizen, he was a Guard. He'd vowed to enforce every rule and regulation they had in place. If I could have bored holes in his skull with my disdain, I would have.

Beckett didn't find me as hard to read as I found him, apparently, and he challenged me even further.

"You think hiding away and barely surviving on whatever you can trade or steal—"

"I don't steal."

"Fine, whatever you can trade, but still, it doesn't make you any less of a subject of their oppression. How much of your life was spent in hiding? How much was spent in fear of being caught?" He raised his eyebrow in a cocky know-it-all gesture that made me wish I had my spear.

"I may be in hiding but at least I don't spend my days sending innocent people to work camps just because they don't want to marry a stranger." My voice shot up an octave and my fists shook.

"To be fair, there are people who want to be together and Match. It's all in the genes."

"I'm not having this conversation with you. You're so deep in it, you don't even know how wrong it is."

"I know it didn't mean shit for my happiness. Don't sell me short, Cressenda, I'm not a fool. I just don't think you're any more free than I am."

His words sank in with frightening clarity. I'd based my entire definition of freedom on who I married—or didn't marry, to be exact. I'd told myself it was worth it to live in solitude and fight for survival, but Beckett's poignant reflections left me wondering.

"So I'll leave you to that little breakdown you're having there." He left me on the sofa and opened a trunk set at the foot of his bed. Two white-cased pillows and a thick brown blanket transformed the sofa into an opulent bed, the likes of which I hadn't seen since my childhood. Try as I might to refuse the amenities, I couldn't resist the opportunity to sleep in such comfort.

I melted into the warmth, pulling the blanket up tight under my chin. One last survey of Tilo and Tonk proved to be unnecessary as they lay cuddled up on the ridiculous fur rug, content and relaxed. Beckett sat on the floor near the boys, reading on his holo-tab and sipping more tea. The entire scene was so serene, I felt as if I had fallen into a dream that I never wanted to wake from. The beautiful fire, my happy boys, and a place that felt like home. My eyes fluttered shut despite my fight to keep them open. The last thing I remembered was what felt oddly like Beckett tucking the blanket in around my arms before I fell into a deep sleep.

CHAPTER FIVE
Inside These Walls

When Beckett finally awoke, I stood staring out the window, contemplating how to take the boys out in the storm. They needed to go outside, sooner rather than later, and relieve themselves.

"Are you thinking of leaving?" He sat up in his bed, the blankets bunched in his lap and leaving his chest fully exposed. He didn't seem the least bit uncomfortable baring his skin in my presence. His hair, unruly and messy from sleep, softened his edges. I could see the boy he was in his youth. I shied away and turned my attention back out the window.

"I need to get the boys out there. They can only hold it so long."

He scratched at his unshaven face while he considered my current predicament.

"It looks like there is only about three feet of snow right now. I think I can get them out there if I dig out the door." I glanced at him, still lazing in his bed, arms stretched up high above him.

"Are you crazy?" Beckett rubbed his eyes and threw off the covers. Much to my relief, and a bit of dismay, he wore a pair of well-worn flannel pajama pants. He might have worked for the enemy but that didn't negate his undeniable good looks.

"I'm not crazy. You have any better ideas?" As if to punctuate the time sensitive nature of this necessity, Tilo paced at the door and let out a whine. "I'm going." I had one foot strapped into the snowshoes perched at the door when Beckett yanked the other one out of my hand.

"You're the most incorrigible woman on the planet. Gimme those," he said, already dressed in his insulated pants and coat. He finished lacing his boots and grumbled while he strapped on the snowshoes.

When the access door slid open, I was relieved to find the snow hadn't fallen so heavily that we couldn't get through the door. Beckett shoveled a small path away from the entrance for the boys. We both stood in the doorway watching as they jumped through the deep piles of powder-light snow. Beckett went to the kitchen and filled two mugs with sweet spiced tea and soy milk, handing me one upon his return. We laughed and smiled at the sight of Tilo disappearing under the snow, then popping to the surface and shaking snow off his fur in a giant cloud of white flakes. I found it endearing that he enjoyed Tonk and Tilo's frolicking. I wondered if he was lonely without a pack of his own to keep him company. It occurred to me that he lived an oddly solitary life for a citizen in the Collective.

I called the boys in and parceled out some animal rind that had been in the pack on the sled. They returned to their spot on the fur rug at the foot of the hearth and chewed with the beautiful single-mindedness that belonged solely to the animal conscience.

Beckett hung back in the kitchen, shifting his weight from foot to foot, staring in the cabinets.

"So, you hunt, huh? You're kind of small for a hunter."

"It's less about size and more about skill. I'm guessing you wouldn't know that, though."

He shot me a look over his shoulder and turned his attention back to the sparse pantry. I didn't know how this man stayed alive all this time by himself. He'd never make it as an Outlier.

"I'll do it." I moved around him, pulling out a few ingredients and giving him my best disapproving once-over while setting them in front of him. "Go over there, you're in the way."

He watched from the table as I prepared us a small breakfast. We ate in relative silence, chewing slowly and deliberately. Knowing there was nowhere to go, no way to escape the confines of the cabin, the need to make our meal fill an infinite amount of time was like a cord pulled tight around our necks, threatening to become a noose to either of us if our current situation went awry.

I regretted all the times at home when I'd lamented not having one of the fancy power dishwashers the Citizens had, because right then I would have given a week's worth of grain to have the time-consuming job of washing our dinner dishes by hand. He led me through placing the dishes into the washer one at a time with precision and care, explaining how to prevent overcrowding and an inferior wash cycle. We concentrated heavily on the task and tried hard not to look directly at the other's eyes when speaking.

I realized halfway through breakfast that every time our eyes met, my stomach flipped and my skin tingled. Dangerous energy crackled between us. Sexual encounters outside of a Match were strictly forbidden. I couldn't imagine Beckett would let that happen, though, being a man of the law. No good could come from letting my body get carried away and enticing my mind into places that were nothing but a dead end.

I spent several hours staring out the window, with Tilo by my side, while Tonk continued to rest and recuperate. His wound was healing much faster than it would have at home. The rapid recovery startled me when I changed his dressing and applied more ointment. Scientifically-engineered medicines worked well and they worked fast. As much as I hated the Affinity, the benefits of their scientific advancements didn't escape me.

Beckett pretended not to watch me, peeking up from his holo-tab from time to time. I hadn't done anything interesting in the hours that passed and I took great satisfaction in knowing he needed to occupy himself with the electronic tethers of technology while I sat content with the freedom of the day.

In the afternoon, music filled the uncomfortable space between us. I scanned through hundreds of songs on his holo-tab, eventually selecting a list of amazing tunes from times gone by. We found common ground in our love for Green Age sounds made with instruments as opposed to the digital contortion known as music in the modern world.

"How did you find this music? I thought only eccentric old citizens longing for the Green Age still listened to this," I teased him, his preference for the Green Age clear in everything in his home from the pillows to the color on the walls. Actually, the fact that he had any color on the walls at all was unusual for a home in the Collective. Citizens preferred modern, industrial materials and utilitarian design. No stylization, no personality, and certainly no fluffy green pillows and golden-hued walls.

"Everything is available in digi-file; you just have to know where to look for it." He smirked, hinting at some secret digital knowledge.

"You also need one of these special issue tablets from the Affinity, but, you know, no big deal." I laughed at my own sarcasm and stuck my tongue out at him. Beckett tried to look annoyed but his face resembled that of an adult trying not to entertain the smart remarks of a petulant child.

I lounged on the sofa while he fitted himself into the far corner where his mattress met the wall. Music floated all around us, bouncing off the walls and making the air heavy with beautiful color and emotion. One of the songs on the list featured a gorgeous falsetto male voice layered on top of thunderous drums and a driving bass guitar. I closed my eyes and let the music completely sweep me away.

Beckett noticed my abandon and increased the volume so loud I couldn't hear myself think. Music came blaring through the speakers expertly placed throughout the cabin. I'd never been immersed in sound like that before. Even in my youth, I hadn't experienced the consumption of my mind and body within melody. Everything outside of this room, these four walls, everything waiting for me over the mountain and deep in the forest, it all disappeared. All that I could think or feel was the rhythm in the music. My heart followed the sultry pace of the bass and my chest constricted with the painful lyrics bleeding out of the soulful singer.

The song ended and I shot up from my prone position, finding Beckett smiling at me from across the room as the beginning notes of the same decadent music filled the cabin again. I returned a grateful smile and sank back into the overstuffed cushions beneath me. As I lay, swept away in the power of the song, I felt Beckett watching me. I opened my eyes and met his in a gratuitous appraisal of my body, stretched out as if it were on display for him. Our exchange felt right, not dirty or salacious at all, just one person enjoying the vision of another person in complete physical and emotional rapture. We were happy there together, in that moment.

As the last note sounded, I immediately wished I could hear it again. If I could have bottled the feeling of that song, of our shared experience of pure bliss, I would have in a second. The remainder of the day, Beckett and I let the bleat of the horns, the sigh of the strings, and the pounding of the percussion fill up all the empty space around us.

***

When evening fell, we turned on the Affinity Broadcasting Channel and watched the daily address from the Council. Three men with strong jaws, high cheekbones, and wide masculine brows wearing shiny suits spoke of "greater good" and "prolific life", emphasizing the benefits such practices provided to all of humankind. I couldn't believe the rhetoric hadn't been updated in ten years.

"Still the same old bullshit," I said as I took the scraps of my dinner to the boys.

Beckett pursed his lips and knotted his brow, again. I still hadn't worked out exactly what it meant when he looked at me like that. Whether concern or consternation, the feeling plagued him regularly. The two moons were already in the sky and darkness enveloped the night. Snow piled high as the storm gained momentum and continued to dump inch after inch, foot after foot of frigid crystal flakes.

"Why don't you have any Christmas decorations up in here?"

He stood and ran his hand along the mantel, tracing the ornate curved lines at the corners and long straight lines in between. I observed his melancholy demeanor from my regular spot on the sofa.

"We used to decorate the house. A tree with some ribbons tied to it sat in the corner over there." He gestured to the dark corner of the cabin near the kitchen. "Marielle had cut these angels with trumpets out of red cloth. They were all attached to each other, flipping back and forth, and she'd string them across this wall. And here," he tapped on the mantel as he spoke, "is where she'd put all the snow globes." A sad smile haunted his face.

"That sounds pretty." I wanted to know more. His words revealed the small details of his past, but his eyes and the sorrow in his voice hinted that his pain came from more than just losing a wife who made cute paper angels.

"Pretty. Yes, it was pretty. She was good at that, at making things pretty."

"Why don't you have them up now? I could help, if you like."

"I don't have the stuff anymore. I tried to use it all the first Christmas after she died. I felt ridiculous hanging on to the stupid traditions of the past. Christmas was Marielle's thing, not mine."

I wanted to hold him in my arms and rub his head until the creases and the tension all melted away. Guilt bound itself around my gut until I gave in and accepted that the sorrow was not mine but his own to conquer. "I'm sorry, I shouldn't have asked."

"It's okay. I always thought it was a waste to perpetuate the folklore of Christmas. She got really into it, you know? It was a big deal to her, but it's just another day to me." He chuckled lightly and added, "She used to play these old, old songs, where people sang about the beauty of winter and celebrating snow. Can you imagine that? A time where snow was something special."

My heart sank. Beckett lived a solitary, empty existence, even more so than me in my lonely cabin in the middle of the forest. Uneasy silence hung around us. Searching for the right words, I knew the brutal honesty that stirred on the tip of my tongue would be of no help to our situation. Against my better judgment, I let the words fall out of my mouth.

"It's not just another day. It's Christmas. Don't you believe in the magic of Christmas?"

He answered me with the arch of a single eyebrow and an accompanying smirk. I sighed in exasperation. Would every one of our conversations become a battle of wits?

"I'm not talking about religion, because who does that anymore? I'm talking about the spirit of it all. One time, every year, where families come together and celebrate their love and gratitude for each other. One day where people take a break from thinking about their own wants and focus on the needs of others. I think it's the most beautiful time of year."

Beckett picked up my feet, sat near me on the sofa, and deposited them back in his lap. I drew my legs into my body and wedged myself into the far corner opposite him. He frowned and stretched his arms along the back and the arm of the sofa.

"I haven't had any reason to celebrate in ten years. I usually don't even realize it's Christmastime unless I make a trip in to the Collective." I added, "You shouldn't take it for granted."

We fell back into silence, me huddled in the corner of the sofa and him with his thoughts etching deep grooves in his forehead. I left him on the sofa with his thoughts and joined Tilo and Tonk on the fur rug. Distance helped ease the uncomfortable silence between us.

I laid with the boys on the floor near the crackling wood fire, stroking and petting them. I understood why they spent their time cuddled up on the white fur rug. It was almost as if the rug, the warm yellow and orange light the fire cast, and the peace of the timelessness of our stay transported us to another time. A time when life moved more slowly and the fight for survival didn't overshadow every minute of every day.

Hours passed in silence. I remained on that rug, turning my life and my choices repeatedly over in my mind. What if I came back to the Affinity? There were rumors of Outliers returning, serving small sentences in camps as a penance, and being allowed to join the Collective again. They were Matched, of course, providing they were still of childbearing age. Life in the Collective had its perks. Would it really be that bad to be Matched?

What of my parents? Of everything they gave up, including their freedom, so that I learned to be self-sufficient? So that I wouldn't be forced to have children for the "good of the human race."

No, even with all the conveniences and consolations handed out by the Affinity, I knew

I couldn't return to a life that was not my own. Tears slipped from the corners of my eyes, disappearing into my hair, leaving a trail of wet evidence as they rolled across my skin.

Beckett's large frame came into my line of sight. He crouched next to me. Reflexively, I turned away. He took it as an invitation to make himself comfortable and stretched his long legs out opposite my body.

"Are you missing your family?" His voice didn't waver, even in the intrusiveness of such a personal question.

"Why do you assume you know what I'm thinking? It's none of your business, anyway." I wanted him to move away from me and let me have my sorrow in private.

He laughed, deep and strong. I loved the way it sounded and I hated the way it made me feel. My heart fluttered as he rubbed his hand up and down the arm that faced him. I flipped back over, pushing all my anger out at him with a nasty sneer on my face. He laughed harder.

"How dare you laugh at me!" I sat up, enraged, wishing we weren't barricaded in by four feet of snow and there was somewhere, anywhere, for me to escape.

"Cressenda, it's written all over you. Every thought you have, everything you feel, you wear your emotions like armor. How could I not know what you're thinking?"

"Don't touch me. I can't stand being mocked. Your patronizing nice-guy act is really offensive."

He responded as if I'd slapped him across the face. His hand jerked back and his posture stiffened. "You've been here an entire day and still don't find any part of me trustworthy. Have you considered that maybe I *am* just a nice guy?" He stood from the floor and sat on the sofa with a frustrated huff.

"I still don't understand why you brought me here. What's in this for you?"

"Why does there have to be something in it for me? I'm just trying to save your life." Anger threatened to spill out of him.

"It doesn't make any sense. I'm no one to you. Nothing. Just another Outlier breaking rules and hiding from the Affinity. You should be turning me in, not saving me."

"You don't know me at all," he whispered and shook his head.

"You're right, I don't know you, so why should I trust you?" I hollered at him, fed up with our redundant game of twenty questions. I found myself standing, hunched forward, angry and aggressive. I stared hard at Beckett, waiting for him to reply with his own fiery gaze, but he relaxed further into the sofa.

"You've been living by yourself out there in the wild for too long. You can't tell when someone cares about you, even when they're standing right in front of you."

Beckett's words stopped my anger from reaching its pinnacle. The idea that he could care for me, enough to risk his livelihood and his standing with the Affinity, made my heart skip a beat. I moved from the floor and sat close to him on the sofa, tucking my legs underneath me, feeling the slight sting of defeat mixed with confusion and caution.

"You're right, it's been a long time since I've had anyone care about me. It feels good to be here with you. Too good. I wish I could stay here in this bubble with you, but reality is right outside that door and its coming for me."

Beckett wrapped his fingers around mine and pulled me against him. We sat like that, my head on his shoulder, both watching the fire flicker and the wood crackle, for what might have been hours.

My eyelids grew heavy and my breathing slowed. The steady rhythm of his breath lulled me closer and closer to sleep. He startled me when he spoke.

"Can't you just accept my generosity and stop second-guessing everything I do?"

I turned my head to look him dead in the eye and answered him with the deepest sincerity when I said, "No."

The color in his cheeks brightened as his anger flared. In a flash of movement, his thick arms wrapped around my body and he pressed his mouth to mine. The feeling of his lips, firm and confident against mine, was exquisite. I kissed him back with enthusiasm and crawled onto his lap. His hands smoothed the tension from my back in even, gentle strokes. I molded myself to him, deepening the kiss and closing any distance between us.

Our kisses were desperate, searching for the same heat that flowed from the hearth, for the comforts of home and love, longing for it to melt our frozen hearts. Beckett broke the kiss and placed feather light kisses along my jaw and down the side of my neck. The teasing touch of his lips against my delicate skin ratcheted up the ache building between my legs. I pulled his head to my throat, wanting more, soaking in every tender kiss. When he got to the sensitive spot where my neck met my shoulder, he flicked his tongue out like a devilish serpent sent to destroy my self-control.

I let out a moan and ground myself against his lap. The erotic feel of his hard length against my heated sex broke our lust-induced haze. Snapped back into reality, we acknowledged this new dangerous territory. Neither of us spoke. We peeled ourselves apart, lying down alongside each other on the sofa. Not willing to let go of the rope swiftly pulling us into treacherous waters, we continued to explore the feel of each other's body, the taste of each other's mouth, and the scent of each other's skin.

We didn't rush through our physical acquaintance, both knowing it shouldn't go any further. Our time together being finite and short lived, I etched each sharp plane of his chest and every bulging curve of muscle in his arms into my memory.

We stayed that way, linked together, holding on to the fire and fulfillment, until the sun peeked over the horizon. Beckett held me tight, the same crease in his brow, when his eyes finally shut. Drifting into unconsciousness after a valiant fight against sleep, I regretted that the night ever had to end. I hoped in the bright light of morning that our weakness remained beautiful and didn't tarnish under the harsh illumination of a new day.

CHAPTER SIX

Fresh Air

I woke to a rush of cold air and the sound of long dragging scrapes. The boys' playful sounds echoed outside of the cabin. I lay alone, wrapped in a heavy comforter, in Beckett's bed with no memory of how I'd got there. Rubbing the sleep from my eyes, I searched the cabin for signs of his whereabouts. The sun shone brightly through the narrow windows and the embers of the previous night's fire glowed in the hearth like red stars in a dark ashen sky.

Beckett's voice seeped through the walls. He spoke to the boys as if he'd known them a lifetime. Still wrapped in the blanket, I grabbed his keycard and walked to the door with a train of green comforter trailing behind me. I opened it just enough to peek at the inconceivable scene that waited for me outside.

Beckett sliced deep into the snow with a shovel, scooping out a huge chunk and tossing it to the side. The wide flat blade cut into the impacted snow without resistance.

"You've made amazing progress. How long have you been out here?"

"Morning, sunshine." He ignored my question, yelling over the constant scraping sound the shovel made against the hard ground.

I cupped my hands around my mouth and asked loudly, "Tea?"

"No, I'm good. I had some earlier." He smiled and waved me off. "Go ahead and turn on the kettle. I'll be done in a bit."

My groggy brain didn't find humor in his jovial demeanor. I slammed my hand against the access door button and made myself at home in his utilitarian kitchen. The very plain cabinetry and counters accompanied by the curious lack of design clashed with the heavily stylized decor of the living area. I realized he seemed to have little cooking knowledge, making the most basic meals when he had taken to the task of feeding us. I contemplated his discomfort with the kitchen while I waited for the kettle to heat.

Returning to the access door with my now-favorite green mug full of steaming tea, I opened it wide, letting the light stream in and fill the cabin. Beckett worked for a few minutes longer. The muscles in the backs of his arms flexed with each thrust of the shovel. He stopped from time to time to wipe at his brow and stretch his arms out at his sides. When he'd finished shoveling a long path through his property, Beckett disappeared into the shed. I called the boys back in and closed the access door, leaving him to whatever privacy he sought out in the cold.

An errant container of granola clusters found in the pantry made a decent breakfast. I drank my tea and had a lengthy one-sided conversation with the boys. Searching for purpose, I emptied the kettle, wiped down the counter, made the bed and adjusted the number on the digital screen of the thermostat. When his visit to the sanctuary dragged on for what seemed like an hour, I helped myself to a shower.

I smiled with relief at the simple control panel installed in Beckett's bathroom. A button that turned water on, one that turned it off, and two buttons to adjust the temperature of the water. Leave it to him to have the most straightforward set up. Beckett liked things clear and concise, that much I could tell. He never minced words and always said, with startling honesty, what he thought. Although there were parts of himself and his past he clearly didn't want to reveal, he was not secretive, just private. Everyone deserved to keep their deepest hurts close to their heart, and as far as I was concerned, Beckett had already shared a large part of his pain with a veritable stranger. I wouldn't search out the root of his pain, for surely it twisted deep inside his soul. Pulling on roots that long and snarled had a tendency to unearth dark truths that no one wanted to face.

I hadn't taken a shower since I was a young girl, and even then only when I had stayed overnight at a friend's house. Most families had bath basins, their function being multifaceted instead of serving one indulgent purpose like a shower stall. Nevertheless, indulge I would. The water streamed hot, leaving long red streaks down my heated skin. Glycerin body wash glided across my skin like silk. Shampoo frothed on my head in a huge crown of bubbles that trailed down my back and pooled at my toes. I felt like a princess in a fairytale from long ago. Having every inch of my body soft and clean was a soothing, albeit foreign, experience. The warmth of the water seeped into my skin, thawing and loosening my muscles.

I let my hands wander along my body, touching and feeling all the places usually locked behind layers of clothing. With my eyes closed and the spray of water tapping against my eyelids in a mirror of my erratic heartbeat, I pressed my fingers firmly against the juncture between my legs. Images of Beckett flashed through my mind. His long, strong arms shoveling snow. The way his large hands wrapped around a mug of tea. Rough stubble scratching across my chin and down the column of my throat. His firm erection pressed against me.

The frightening realization crashed down on me: I wanted Beckett. It was the worst outcome I could have imagined from this crazy experiment of ours. I wanted to feel him move inside me and find out how he fit in the secret parts of my body and my soul. I was desperate to climb inside him, to seek out all of his strengths and his weaknesses, his beautiful lies and his ugly truths, leaving no part of him hidden from my view. I didn't just want his body to be part of mine, although I wanted that very badly. I wanted to know what pained him and gave him that crease in his brow, and what I could do to make him cry out in pleasure.

As I careened toward ecstasy, I bit my lips together to hold back the scream of Beckett's name that accompanied my orgasm. My heart raced from the elation of sexual release and the blinding fear that he might have heard my salacious activity. I leaned my head against the tile of the shower walls. What I felt in my body and in my heart couldn't be dismissed as the foolish desires of a lonely Outlier in need of a good romp in bed. This was the worst kind of naiveté. I was falling in love with the enemy, and I wanted nothing more than for him to love me back.

When I came out of the bathroom, Beckett greeted me with a huge smile and a nervous excitement I hadn't seen in him before. I rubbed the towel through my hair and gave him a sideways glance.

"Uh...what's up? Why're you bouncing around like a kid on Trade Day?" I scanned the room, wondering what had gotten into him.

"You need to dry your hair. Hurry, and I'll show you. We have to go outside and you can't with wet hair. You'll get sick."

He rummaged around in a small closet and pulled out an old hot brush probably left behind by his late wife. Beckett was practically coming out of his skin while he waited for me to finish.

"Are you done yet? C'mon, you're taking so long. How long can it possibly take to dry your hair?"

His childish enthusiasm was almost endearing. Almost. I did a grand flourish as I finished the last section of hair.

His large frame took up the entire doorway. The sheer size of his chest gave my mind ample material for daydreams, like how it might look to have his pecs tensed above me or how he'd fold his massive shoulders as he came. I pushed the sensual thoughts out of my mind and returned the giant grin he had been beaming at me for the last ten minutes.

"Okay, what's all this about? Why are we going outside?"

"You're always so suspicious. Just come out with me. It's not a trick. You're gonna love it."

He rushed to the access door and regally held out his arm in presentation as the door slid open. Outside, parked just in front of the door, sat Beckett's snowmobile, decorated from front to back in red ribbons with sprigs of evergreen branches and shiny silver bells. Tonk and Tilo were in on the surprise as well, it seemed, for they both had red silk ribbons looped through a bell and wrapped around their necks, then tied into crooked, lopsided bows.

"You did this? You put bells on the boys and frilly decorations on your mobile? You've lost your mind. Where did you even get the ribbon? I can't believe it." I aimed to sound pleasantly surprised but came off more like a girl who had just been told she was Matched with the man of her dreams.

"The bells were in the shed for years and the ribbon was on a package I got a few days ago. The tree branches are self-explanatory." He planted his hands firmly on his hips and nodded thoughtfully while he explained how he'd secured everything carefully and how he'd enticed the boys into letting him make them part of the entire ensemble.

"Shall we?"

"Shall we what?"

He didn't think I was going to ride on that death trap, did he? Mobiles moved so fast. They were only machines that followed commands from the driver. I preferred sled teams where you relied on the dogs' instincts as much as your own, if not more. Tonk and Tilo were decorated, but they weren't taking this trip with us.

"C'mon, Cressenda, let's go out and fly through the white nothingness." Laughter belied his desperation for a change of scenery.

I looked over at the boys poised at the access door, observing my reaction and waiting to know if they should escort me back into the house or protect our makeshift home until we returned.

"Oh, what the hell. Let's go!" I bade the boys goodbye and shooed them into the house. Beckett waved his keycard to lock the cabin up tight and turned to me with a sly smile on his lips. Sitting on the back section of the mobile, I wrapped my arms tightly around him. We set off with a jolting start in the direction of the forest's tree-lined edge.

The snow fell slower, lighter than the day before. It was entirely possible that the blizzard had ended, but we couldn't be sure until this evening's address. For now, we enjoyed the yellow sun against the cerulean sky and the shocking white blanket that covered everything around us.

Becket drove the mobile fast and hard, turning sharp at corners and alighting over rock formations like they were built for his amusement and recreation. I hung on to his waist, certain I was crushing the air from his lungs, but unable to let go for fear of being tossed off the seat and into the deep banks of snow that had accumulated over the past two days.

He drove further into the forest, engrossed in an exhilarating game of chicken with the twenty-foot tall trees that grew in eerily uniform lines throughout the forest, a wicked maze of rows and columns all intersecting and overlapping without ever actually closing themselves off. Beckett raced through the forest as if he had done it every day of his life. Maybe he had. Most of Beckett's life was still a mystery to me.

We came to an abrupt halt at the end of a row of bushy trees with silver-tinged needles. Beckett plucked me off the mobile and spun me around once, for good measure, before depositing me back on my feet.

"How awesome was that? I haven't been out for a run like that in forever."

"That was something else, that's for sure. I'm not sure how you didn't kill us, but it was heart-pounding. I think I'll stick to sledding with my boys."

"Have you ever driven one? A mobile, I mean?"

I shook my head and stepped back from the snowmobile as if it was a wild animal.

"It's a lot of power, but I think you'd be fine. You're used to controlling your dogs when you're sledding. This is pretty much the same, but faster. Get on, we'll do a test run."

"I don't think so. What if someone sees us, or worse, if I run someone over? Too dangerous."

"Don't be a coward." He had already figured out what made me tick. *Sneaky bastard.*

"I'm pretty sure you and I both know I'm not a coward." I gave him back the raised eyebrow he so often gave me.

"I dunno, Cressie, you sure look scared of that mobile." The lilt in his voice was obviously meant to tease and taunt. I ignored it, distracted by the casual use of my nickname.

"Why did you call me that?" I folded my arms across my chest and pulled my hood tight around my head. Snow had begun to fall again, a light dusting covering everything around us.

He closed the distance between us and pulled the laces of my hood, knotting them tightly. Beckett left his hood down, unfazed by the falling snow. The white flakes were a sharp contrast as they landed on the curls of his pitch-black hair. His light eyes looked even more brilliant with the warm tone of his dark skin clad in the puffy white coat and standard Affinity issue grey insulated pants.

"Sorry. I didn't mean to make you uncomfortable. It just popped out of my mouth. Should I just call you by your full name...Cressenda?" I could feel the hot puffs of breath on my cheek as each word left his mouth. So close and so quiet, I could hear my body screaming for him.

"No one has called me Cressie since my parents were taken away. It just surprised me. You...you can call me Cressie." I couldn't look at him when I said it. I knew the depths he would search into my soul. That was the thing about Beckett: from the moment I met him, he reached behind my solid walls and touched all the parts of my heart that were withered and neglected.

We stood in the clearing, hidden by tall trees and mountains of snow, daring one another to make the first move. A standoff of wills. After the way I threw myself at him the night before, I didn't have the courage to harness the electricity that arced between us. My body begged and pleaded for him. The air carried the sweet taste of him to my tongue as it passed the short space from his lips to mine. My longing ratcheted up a notch with each intake of breath. Beckett explored every part of my face with steeled scrutiny. Did he see the war that raged inside of me? If so, did he understand it at all?

Much to my relief, Beckett came to me. We shared a long, lingering kiss under the virginal falling snow. He held me by my face, ours bodies still inches apart, and drowned me in chaste kisses that drove my body wild but left my mind open and unguarded. Imagined scenes of a preposterous future flooded my consciousness. Visions of Beckett and me locked in an embrace, images of us hunting side by side, and most painful of all, illusions of us living together happily, building a life in the wilderness.

A sorrowful ache filled my chest. I could never have that with him. We could never be that together. I inhaled deeply, my eyes still closed, and stepped back from the tragically beautiful moment. Hiding the sadness that filled my heart, I splashed a smile across my face.

Nodding in the direction of the snowmobile, I said, "Loser rides on the back."

We raced across the few steps to the mobile, and although Beckett could have beaten me easily, he let me win. Fear of him exposing the feelings growing in my heart far outweighed my trepidation about driving the mobile. He walked me through the startup of the powerful machine and grabbed handles that I hadn't noticed on the sides of the rear seat. I shook my head. *Forgot to mention those, did he?* When I gestured to the handles questioningly, Beckett's only response was a sheepish smirk and a shrug.

The mobile took off smoothly, gliding as if it were on hidden rails beneath us. I didn't speed through the wilderness. Instead, I wanted to see where we were and where we had been. Pink, orange, and purple hues swirled in the sky, taking up more than their share of the horizon. The second moon was rising and dark would be upon us soon. Mustering up some bravado, I pushed the throttle and shot us forward into the great expanse of land that would take us home.

CHAPTER SEVEN
Two Moons, One Sky

Though our trip home offered less exciting travel, the scenery remained spectacular. I knew I would cherish these moments when I returned to my solitary life. Never in my wildest dreams did I think that a blizzard would bring me to a Guard of the Affinity, a Sympathizer no less, who would remind me how to enjoy the presence of another, to indulge in the freedom of frivolity, and to allow the raw emotions of humanity to take root in my heart again.

The boys greeted us with their usual hopping and prancing. A stern look reminded them to control their excitement before I rewarded them with affection. Beckett watched with warmth and caring in his eyes. I waved him over, welcoming him to join our exchange.

"Hi, boys," he said, petting them in long strokes down their sides. He was careful to avoid the bandages on Tonk's ribs.

"I should check his wound, and then I'll feed us all."

Shock and relief overtook me when I removed the bandages and found his injury had almost completely healed. Progress like this would have taken weeks at home with herbal packs and salves. I applied the ointment for what I knew would be the last time and taped on a new bandage only to keep Tonk from licking off the medicine. Beckett sat with the boys on the hideous fur rug while I made the meal I'd promised earlier.

Standing alone in the kitchen, I cooked with a heavy heart. It was clear the blizzard had passed and I would need to leave in the morning. The Collective would soon resume business as usual and I couldn't risk being caught in his home. More important, Beckett couldn't risk being caught with me. Besides, I had a new satchel to sew and hydro-planter to repair.

I steadied my emotions by concentrating on the responsibilities that waited for me at home. As dinner conversation flowed, Beckett listened with rapt attention to my stories of the intricacies of Outlier life. "So you can really grow plants in those contraptions you build? Amazing. Do you grow any of the more fun medicinal stuff?" He wagged his eyebrows at me and I threw a napkin at him.

"Of course not," I said through my laughter. "I wouldn't waste the energy. The herbs are so important to keeping us healthy. Teas and herb packs are crucial to healing infections and curing illnesses."

"And you actually hunt beasts, like, kill them and cut their fur off?" His face scrunched up at the thought.

I explained the multiple uses of a spear, not just for taking down beasts when the opportunity arose but also for fishing in the warmer months, as well as for overall self-defense. I drew diagrams on his holo-tab and taught him how to make his own, step by step. He balked at the idea of using beast claws for spear tips, insisting he could barter for something from the machine traders in the Path.

After dinner, we gravitated to our regular spots on the sofa. Beckett built a large fire, using more wood than I thought was safe, although he assured me the cabin wouldn't burn down while we slept.

"I'm going to miss this. I forgot how beautiful a wood fire could be."

Beckett left his corner of the sofa and leaned closer to me. "You're really going to leave, aren't you?" He didn't look at me when he spoke.

"Of course I am." I couldn't look at him, either. "My life is back at my cabin. What am I gonna do, hide here for the rest of my life? I don't belong here. I have to go home."

Silence stretched long and thin between us. My hand twitched at my side and my feet were restless. Anxiety crept up my spine as I made a mental checklist of everything I had with me. I had to make sure I didn't leave anything behind. Hard as I tried to concentrate on the task, my mind kept returning to Beckett. I hadn't realized the sigh that escaped my lips until Beckett called me out.

"You're sad again. Why are you forcing yourself to go back if it makes you sad?"

"Life is full of sad necessities." I rose and moved to the small dining table in the kitchen. The medic kit sat on the tabletop, mocking my jumbled and confused mind with its neatly arranged rows of vials and tubes. I fingered the ointment that had healed Tonk so quickly. My heart clenched at the reality of the suffering Tonk would have endured if it weren't for our unexpected circumstances.

Life under the Affinity, in the Collective, was easy and safe.

For a moment, I clutched the tube of ointment and let my mind wander. What if I joined the Collective? If I could survive the wild, certainly I could endure a few years in a camp. I had youth on my side. They would be eager to release me and put me on the fast track to reproduction. I probably had a good ten years of childbearing left in me. That could be at least four or five new members of the race to the Affinity. Would Beckett wait for me?

I was fraught with sorrow, knowing even if he waited for me to be released, even if he threw off the stigma of my past as an Outlier, the chances of us being Matched were slim. We could apply to be tested for compatibility, but the statistics didn't fall in our favor. I knew then that a slim possibility of a future with Beckett didn't outweigh the risk of giving up my freedom. Quiet resolve settled though my body as I made the realization that I would be leaving the first person I dared to trust since I'd escaped the world of the Affinity.

Beckett sat in his corner of the sofa, eyes trained on the fire in front of him. I watched with complete and utter heartbreak as he moved off the sofa and knelt between the two sleeping huskies on the floor. Tilo stretched his body out long and exposed his belly to Beckett as he rubbed his hands across their fur in long, affectionate pets.

My feet carried me across the room to him, even as my head begged me to plant my ass firmly on the sofa and leave him to his moment of happiness. I stood behind him, soaking in the beauty of my boys comfortable and content in Beckett's home. Sensing my presence, he turned to me, the same crease drawn on his brow that so frequently disturbed his handsome features.

"You can take the medic kit with you, and anything else you can use."

"That's generous of you, but—"

"Damn it, Cressie, why can't you let me help you? I want to help you." When he turned to me, his eyes were hard. He stomped into the kitchen and yanked a bottle of brown liquid from the highest cabinet, taking a deep pull directly from the opening of the narrow glass neck. He grimaced while he took a short glass from the lower shelf and filled it with more of the alcohol.

I stared, slack-jawed, as he threw back the drink and immediately poured another. Beckett's casual acquaintance with the illegal drink struck me as both shocking and enticing. A glance in my direction told me I wasn't invited to join.

"I'm not asking," I said, gesturing to the bottle.

"I'm not offering." He slammed the cabinet door and stepped wide around me on his way back to the sofa. In all the time he and I had spent locked in the cabin together, it had never felt as small as it did right at that moment. Having had enough of our circuitous argument, I secluded myself in the bathroom. The disproportionately large mirror hanging over the sink painted a vivid picture of how this time spent with Beckett had affected me. My reflection held the image of health and physical strength I hadn't seen since I'd left home as a kid. Bright skin, pink cheeks, clean, and surprisingly well-fed. A smile came easily and worked its way up to the crinkled corners of my eyes. How long would this last? How long until the circles under my eyes returned and my skin turned pale and ashen? How long until the daily fight for survival tore at my skin and deteriorated my organs? Until my health, both physically and emotionally, was in constant jeopardy?

I splashed cool water on my face and pulled the door open, nearly peeing myself when I slammed into a wall of muscle blocking the doorway. Beckett's arms were outstretched on each side, bracing himself between the door jambs. His chest rose and fell with rapid breaths. I watched with cautious concern as he ran his hands up and down the doorframe. His eyes darted around and he licked his lips before he spoke.

"Don't leave yet. Just stay one more day, one more, and maybe we can figure something out. If you go back out there now, I'll never see you again. I won't be able to help you like I can when you're here."

Making him understand why I needed to leave, sooner rather than later, would be a daunting task. The ever-present crease in his forehead aged him while the sadness in his eyes gave him the appearance of a lost little boy. I did the only thing I could. Pressing my body to his with as much force as I could muster, I hugged him. Beckett tried to free himself from my embrace but I held on tighter. Time moved beyond the socially acceptable length of a friendly hug, into that place where you know the intimacy was threatening to well up and overflow, saturating the moment and forcing both people to acknowledge the emotions at hand.

One feather-light touch between our lips turned into furious kisses made up of passion and desperation. I felt him everywhere, his hands on my back, lips pressed to my neck, pelvis pushing against mine, but I still couldn't get close enough to him. Unconscious need led us to his bed. No thoughts entered my mind outside of the driving desire to have Beckett, my lonely savior, understand how much of my heart would stay here with him, forever.

Our movements were a frantic rush of discarded clothes and tangled limbs. I opened my eyes at discordant intervals, blinded by the beauty in our contrasts. His dark skin against my pale flesh, the way his large hands cradled the curve of my bottom, and his vibrant blue eyes begging for more. Knowing this would be both the beginning and the end, I resolved to give Beckett everything I could on our last night.

Pressing him down to lie below me, I straddled his waist and kissed all the tender spots along his neck and chest. Every kiss elicited from him a surrendering sigh. I shifted to place my weight over his hardened length, which was met with a groan of gratitude. I splayed my hands across his chest and wanted to cry at the rush of excitement brought on by the feel of him underneath me. Spurred on by the mutual grunts of approval as our sex ground against each other, I moved between his legs and stripped him of the last piece of cloth that concealed his excitement. His body was as exposed as my emotions felt. I masked my nerves by taking him into my mouth, lavishing attention on him with abandon.

My efforts were rewarded with a deep, hissing, "Yes." His vocalized pleasure acted as tinder to the burning fire in my body. He fought the urge to move, his hands fisting tight into the sheets. One long, languid stroke of my tongue destroyed his resolve and he thrust into my mouth as I enveloped him again. I groaned with satisfaction as he gave up control, but the sound broke his reverie and he sat up on the bed, flipping me over.

"Not time yet, Cressie. I want to feel you come for me, then I'll let go."

Time stood still as Beckett fed all of my desires with passionate aggression. Every place he touched on my flesh removed a corresponding brick from my wall of protection. His fingertips and tongue wove a tapestry across my body, telling a story of trust and love, all the while winding the coil of tension in my belly. I wanted to believe the feeling behind the touch.

The pleasure was so great, so high, I whispered prayers that he would never stop.

He moved on top of me, his weight heavy and pleasing between my legs. Eyes squeezed shut and muscles taut, I knew he was searching for the words to ask.

"Don't stop. I want to feel you." I gripped his erection to punctuate my plea.

He pushed into me and I kissed him hard in response. My mind swirled with pleasure, riddled by images from our past two days together. The rhythm of our conversations across the cold aluminum kitchen table. Steaming mugs of tea in front of the hearth while the passion pulled taut between us. The way I'd felt when I first saw him in the Trade Path. Beckett was everything I hated and everything I hoped for in one delicious package.

Every push he gave was met with my pull. In all the hours we'd spent wrapped in the presence of one another, neither one had given up control, and even now we were fighting for it still. The heat that drew us near the surface of our lust was now the fuel that drove our insatiable need to be connected. I clawed at his back, fighting to feel him under my skin. His arms held me like a vice and brought me close as I struggled to meld my skin to his. My flesh blended with his to make the perfect shade of creation.

"Let me take it from you. Be mine," I said as I moved to climb on top of him again. Much to my relief, Beckett lifted himself off me and eased onto his back instead of fighting me. The sight of him below me, his neck straining in tortured pleasure with his hands anchored on the rounded flesh of my hips as I took in his entire length, was one I wanted burned into my retinas. I wanted to see him painted on the backs of my eyelids when I closed my eyes at night.

A searing heat, like the strike of sulfur on the tip of a match, ignited the fuse in my sex. Fire shot through me until the tips of my fingers tingled and my toes curled. When my boiling blood returned to a simmer, I redoubled my efforts to bring Beckett the same fiery release. Rocking and grinding, I worked until I drove him to the brink. I saw the moment he relinquished his control and let the orgasm rush through his body, the thread of pretense snapping with finality, left to dangle in the air between us as a reminder of who we were supposed to be.

We lay breathless and quiet, a tangle of arms and legs, of fear and feeling. The deep echo of bells sounded in the distance.

"Cressie?"

"Hmm?"

"Merry Christmas."

I laced my fingers through his and looked up at him, defeated by the sorrow-filled satisfaction I found in his eyes.

"Merry Christmas," I replied.

CHAPTER EIGHT
Leaving Love

We lost ourselves in the feel of our heightened longing over and over again, chasing the darkness and running from the inevitable. Every time I began to dose off, Beckett worked to coax another orgasm from me, sometimes with languid, tired limbs, other times in a frantic explosion of desire. I'd lost count of the number of times our bodies shared ecstasy.

When the first sliver of sunlight fought its way onto the horizon, I felt the undertow of sleep threatening to drown me in unconsciousness. Beckett woke me again, but this time his words shocked me into an alert panic.

"I had a sister." His voice was hoarse and dry, adding to the raw feel of his admission.

I didn't speak. I didn't move. I barely let myself breathe. My mind raced in competition with my heart for the answers at the end of the long tunnel of questions stretched out before me.

"I was fourteen when she ran away, three weeks after her sixteenth birthday. They found her body two months later. She was so thin I thought she must have starved to death, but the official report said she died from hypothermia."

My heart shattered into jagged and sharp splinters, slicing and tearing at the inside of my chest. I squeezed his hand and stifled the tears that threatened to spill down my face.

"You kind of remind me of her. Hardheaded and stubborn. She had long hair, too, almost as dark as yours but not your brown eyes, they were light, like mine. It was the only thing about us that showed that we were related. Liana was so much smaller than me, people always thought I was her older brother. It really pissed her off," he finished with a slight chuckle at the memory of her feisty persona.

His mood turned serious and he searched my eyes for answers we both already knew.

"What if you die out there, Cressenda? Nobody will know. Nobody will find you. I won't even know if you made it back home."

"Hey," I said, softening my words, the way one did when the truth was too painful for both the listener and the speaker, "I've been doing this for a long time. I know what I need to do to survive."

"Stay here. Just for another week. Maybe we can find an answer."

"You know what would happen as well as I do. I'd be put in a camp for who knows how long, and when they finally let me out I'd be Matched."

The crease in his brow returned at my mention of being Matched. Neither of us spoke, mulling over the truths and their contrast against our dreams. I had become accustomed to letting go of things in my life, but Beckett...he hadn't been given a choice. As much as he believed I would be yet another person being taken from him against his will, Beckett didn't understand how much of myself I'd be leaving here in this pretty cabin at the edge of the forest.

His caresses became grabs as he was overcome with grief. I placed a chaste kiss on his chattering mouth, the chill of adrenaline that accompanies fear and panic rippling through him. Sadness had taken hold of his sensibility, his actions frantic and disjointed. Open-mouthed kisses along my jaw and a pressing need at my center were his pleas for salvation. Despite the soreness from our marathon lovemaking, I accepted him inside in hope of easing some of his pain.

My misguided attempt at calming him only added to his delirium. He pumped erratically, his mind completely disconnected from his body.

"Don't go. Stay with me. Let me save you." His mournful pleas pressed the shards of my broken heart deeper into my already aching chest.

His grip tightened with each cry for me to stay. I knew his fingerprints would be marked across my ribs in the morning. I had to bring him out of the darkness of his memories before this train of emotion derailed completely.

"Beckett. Beckett, stop. Beckett, baby, look at me. Stop. Not like this. Don't let this be our last memory." I grabbed his face and forced him back to the present.

"Oh, Cressie, I'm so sorry. Did I hurt you? Please, God, tell me I didn't hurt you." His eyes were wild and unfocused.

With soft kisses and murmurs telling of my safety and contentment, he slowly came back from the pit of despair. We didn't talk any more; we simply sat with the sadness of our reality until the second moon disappeared and the sun dominated the sky once again.

"It's time."

He didn't protest when I dragged my exhausted body from the warmth of his bed. I did my best to avoid his gaze as I packed the few belongings I had scattered throughout the cabin. We carried my possessions, along with the medic kit he insisted I take back with me, out to the shed where my sled had been hidden.

That fateful day seemed so long ago. A lifetime of experiences, full of everything and nothing, had happened in the three short days I had been here. A million possibilities played out in my mind of how things would have and could have been so different. Every decision I'd made that day inevitably led me here, to this cabin, where my life changed forever in both good ways and bad.

The sight of Beckett's mobile, still decorated with ribbons and bells, reminded me of the beauty that came with sharing your days with another. I became acutely aware of my impending solitude. The tendrils of loneliness wiggled their way back into my body and searched out the spots where they would bind themselves around my heart and soul again. I let them take hold, knowing my fate was sealed.

Tonk and Tilo followed with slow steps, a blatant expression of their unwillingness to leave. The boys showed Beckett halfhearted displays of affection and he returned the sentiment. I harnessed them to the sled and checked our water supply. When I ran out of things to check and tie down, I faced Beckett.

I wanted to leave him with confidence that I would be fine. I knew I would continue to survive in the wild, but his doubt colored every smile he forced on his lips. So I made him a promise I had no idea whether or not I'd be able to keep.

"I'll come to the Trade Path every other month. We can't talk to each other, obviously, but you'll see me. You'll see that I'm all right and that you have nothing to worry about. I'm gonna be fine out there. I always have been."

His eyes brightened at the prospect of physical evidence of my wellbeing. I had serious concerns about committing to that huge trek over the mountain on a bimonthly basis, but Beckett needed something to hold on to. I would try, for him.

"Well, better get out there. I need to get to the top of the mountain today."

"Cressenda, I just want you to know..." He rubbed the back of his neck and frowned at his boots.

"I already do. You don't need to tell me." I shoved my boots into the braces and yelled to the boys, "Go."

I didn't look back as we pulled away from the cabin. Not as we hit the trail up the mountain, nor when I set up our camp for the night. But in the quiet of the dark night sky, my sore body and exhausted mind won out. I let the anger at Beckett, at myself, and at the world for the shitty circumstances of our predicament, come pouring out of me in a string of obscenities and curses until I ran out of words and energy, falling asleep under the two moons' light.

***

The journey home was quiet. A heavy drapery of white blanketed everything before me and all that lay behind me. Barely visible, thick-barked tree trunks spotted the great expanse of silence. Needled branches hung heavy with the weight of our endless winter. If I hadn't been so well versed in the mountain's terrain I may never have found my way home, for every trace of a path or trail had been obliterated by the blizzard.

I appreciated the quiet. Time and space helped to clear Beckett from my mind. It gave me the opportunity to prepare myself for the long stretches without human contact. Tonk had no trouble with the physical demands of our trek. As much as I tried to ignore it, the fact remained that we owed our good fortune to the Affinity. It infuriated me, it frustrated me, and it weakened my resolve. I had to remind myself, even though my heart could reconcile Beckett's position in the Affinity with his care and concern for me, my head knew better: It wasn't safe for me there. He wanted to protect me, but that would have proven to be an impossible feat within the confines of the Collective. No, my safety belonged to me and only me. I would not give that up to anyone.

Spotting my cabin in the distance, I drove the boys harder, eager to resume my normal life. The three of us collapsed at the access door, catching our breath before we broached the threshold of our reality. I rose to my knees and shoveled the feet of powdery light snow away with my hands. I pushed open the entrance, expecting to be disillusioned with our meager shelter by the time we had spent reveling in the comfortable amenities of the Collective.

What I was met with defied rational logic. Staring into the cabin, it felt as if it went on forever. A long tunnel of empty aluminum and silicone adorned with industrial coils and wiring. Had I been living like this the whole time? No life, no heart existed in this place I had called my home for the past ten years. The cabin was a hollow shell, with only muffled echoes of humanity in its haphazardly placed cot and misshapen table with only one seat. Tilo, Tonk, and I passed through the access door into a void of nothingness. My life of freedom no longer felt untethered. The sickening realization spread though me that I had built my own coffin with tools disguised as independence and ingenuity.

Determined to regain some semblance of normalcy, I unpacked the few things that came home with us and began the process of thawing our cabin. It needed to be comfortable before nightfall, and the second moon already crested the horizon.

Iron coils mounted to the cabin wall, made to mimic a hearth, glowed burnt orange and black, their color a weak substitute for the real thing. I passed the last hour of twilight aligning connections and soldering filament. When the light became too scarce to see, I gave up on the project knowing I had no seeds to plant in the new hydro-grower anyway.

Between the frigid temperatures and the minute ministrations of my work, my fingers had grown cold. I cupped my hands and blew on them while I heated up the kettle. Some toasted quinoa and a nice tea would be the right way for the boys and me to settle in for the night.

Getting back to our natural rhythm would feel right.

Only the boys weren't interested. Instead of coming to the table and waiting for their shares, they stayed on their beds near the heating coils. They had no pretenses, no reason to hide the way they felt. As their leader, they would do what I told them to, but they didn't have to like it. While I fought so hard to bury the feelings I had about our time with Beckett, they openly expressed their mourning at the loss of his company. The best I could offer them was the last few strips of dried rind from our travels in an attempt to comfort them. Neither Tilo nor Tonk even sniffed the gnarled pieces of fat. I sighed and returned to my now cold meal and tepid tea.

I choked down the grain without tasting it, my only goal being to fill my belly and end the day. A new morning would shed light on the beauty of my simple life and remind me of the pleasures that came with providing for oneself. I had to adjust and find hope again, or I might not survive out here on my own anymore.

I made sure the boys were comfortable in their beds and crawled onto my cot. Sleep came quickly and without the excitement of dreams, my mind too tired from the unusual course of events and the physical exertion of our return. Though nightfall brought with it the harsh tones of solitude, the shock of waking up in my cabin instead of in front of Beckett's wood-burning hearth proved to be the hardest part of all.

***

Days passed by, one after the next, and our routine fell into place as if we'd never diverted from our path. Tonk showed no signs of any permanent damage from his injury. Tilo returned to his boisterous and playful self. Things were as they should be and we were content in our home again.

The new hydro-grower sat proudly on the makeshift counter I'd built in the corner of the cabin that served as our kitchen. The addition of some amenities, fashioned after those common to homes in the Collective, helped to give our home new life. Days turned to weeks, weeks turned to months, and before I knew it, my supplies were near depletion again.

Without enough grain and salt to make it another month, I had to brave a trip back to the Collective. Anxiety niggled its way into my gut at the thought of seeing Beckett. The memory of his large frame accentuated in the form-fitting gray and white Affinity uniform remained crystal clear. But the secrets beneath his exterior were the most dangerous threat to my resolve. I adopted a mantra predicated on one simplistic fact: Anonymity protects us both. Any sign that we knew each other would bring too much attention to me, and to him, which could mean disastrous consequences for either of us.

After the ritualistic checking of the pack, the sled, and the harnesses, I forced myself into bed and tried to wrestle my nerves into submission in hope of a few precious hours of rest.

I stared at the ceiling, flat on my back in my cot, with Tonk and Tilo nestled at my side. I couldn't tell if they missed him as much as I did or if they were simply in tune with my sullen emotions. How could three days have changed my life so drastically? Beckett was unlike any member of the Affinity I had ever met. My mind played back over everything I could have done differently. If only I would have given up on finding a trade for my tea leaves. If I hadn't argued with the silicone trader, if I had just moved on, the grungy Outlier boy wouldn't have grabbed my satchel and Beckett wouldn't have intervened. I went round and round in my head, but the answer remained the same. My life was easier, uncomplicated, and safer before I fell in love with Beckett.

Accepting the fact that sleep was not coming, I heaved my weary body from the cot and paced the dusty cabin floor. Eventually I found myself sitting in the lone seat that accompanied my table, staring at nothing, daydreaming about Beckett.

Lost in a reverie of images of his chest hovering above me, of his hand on my hip, of his tantalizing whispers against my skin, my cheeks flushed with embarrassment even though no one was there to see. I ran my hands up and down the length of my arms trying to rub out the goose bumps. Another memory of his lips trailing down my stomach brought a fresh chill. I forced myself from my stool to turn up the heating element.

I longed for the beautiful log-fueled hearth that had enveloped me while in the safe hideaway of his cabin. The rich smell of wood smoke still permeated my clothing, bringing a mix of sentimental feelings from childhood and sensual memories of being held in Beckett's arms. I increased the number on the digital screen and settled in front of the iron hearth, knowing it still wouldn't bring the warmth I craved. For the first time since my parents were taken by the Affinity, I felt the extreme cold of our frozen environment in every part of my body. Not just in my fingers or my toes, not in the frost against my skin, but deep in every fiber of my body. The very air that filled my lungs stung, frigid and biting. It hurt to draw it in, to try to sustain on it, and found it even more excruciating to force it back out.

I stood, chasing the warmth that floated from the glowing orange coils in front of me. The change made the pain worse instead of better. The wafting hot air wrapped around me, restraining and restricting my lungs even more as I inhaled. I moved across the room, searching for cleansing breaths. The tightness in my chest intensified, causing fear to spiral in my mind. Panic rose from the base of my spine and I clutched at my throat. The boys closed in around me, their instinct telling them to protect me from the invisible assailant.

Instead of quelling my fear, their presence only intensified my suffocation. I ran, fumbling, to the access door and slammed my hand against the button until it jerked open. Out in the snowy expanse, I gasped and sucked at the open air, falling to my knees as I succumbed to the knowledge that it wasn't the air in my cabin, nor the air out in the wild, that was insufficient. Beckett had breathed new life into my soul, and without him there was no air.

I screamed out into the desolate white landscape, causing a lone owl to flee from the disruption. For the first time in ten years, I gave myself over to the loneliness and the sorrow, crying tears for everything I had lost, for everything that had been taken from me, and for the unending isolation that served as the price of freedom. The beautiful enticements of liberty lost their charm if the cost was love. My parents gave up everything to avoid me being Matched, but they hadn't fully considered what an alternative life of solitude would mean for me.

The wracking sobs subsided, but the tears continued to fall silently in fat, wet drops down my face. Exhaustion overtook my limbs. I felt as if gravity had tripled its force, weighing me down heavier with each step back into the cabin. Tonk and Tilo shook out their fur and gently nudged me through the door. I cranked the thermostat up as high as I could and climbed into my cot. Instead of curling up on their beds, the boys snuggled in on both sides of me. I hoped between the blazing heat of the electric coils and the crowded bodies on my bed, I'd find some warmth to drive out the sadness that had settled over my heart.

CHAPTER NINE
Finding Each Other

Accents of green dotted across white as it rushed by, and purple turned to pink before giving itself over completely to blue in the dense winter sky. Although the shortest day of the year had passed, the boys and I were still in a race against the short-lived daylight. Tilo accepted the breakneck pace of our travel with his usual jovial nature, but Tonk's greater wisdom meant he understood the stakes at hand.

He pressed onward and upward, against the thinning air and the building anxiety.

I stopped at regular intervals during our ascent up the mountain, but only long enough to catch our breath and rehydrate, then we resumed our climb. Instead of the setbacks we had faced on our last trip, our journey continued without interruption. I couldn't help but feel like Fate had taken our side for once. At every stop, I checked on the medic kit I'd brought with us, grateful that we hadn't needed it but acutely aware of the danger we'd narrowly escaped without it last time.

The sky shone clear and the winds were calm. We crested the peak in record time and I made the aggressive decision to continue down the mountain until nightfall. A good two hours of daylight remained and I refused to waste them.

The blessedly unmarred trail down the mountain enabled our quick descent. As the sun dipped into the horizon, we ended our travels for the day. I chose a heavily wooded area to set up our camp for the night. The boys and I fed on granola and a few strips of dried meat before huddling together under the shelter of trees and our thermo-blankets.

I slept restlessly, anxious to get to the Trade Path and face the memories that had been haunting me. Though I was confident that Beckett, if he hadn't already been reassigned for his error of letting an Outlier slip away, wouldn't turn me in when he saw me, the other Guard who'd seen me remained a viable threat.

We woke before the sun was up and set back out on the trail immediately. The last few hours were spent trudging through knee-high snow and it proved to be taxing on our already drained bodies. The dogs were nearly covered in some deeper sections and I knew they were getting uncomfortable being immersed in snow for so long. I made the uneasy decision to head west and enter the Collective through the far end, the very part of the forest where Beckett's home was located. It was the only part of the mountain that didn't have a steep grade and would be much less physically demanding.

The taxing rate of our hurried travel finally caught up with Tonk and Tilo. They couldn't continue to pull the sled without injury. As much as I didn't want to visit the places that still lived vividly in my dreams and opened fresh wounds on a nightly basis, I knew it had to be done.

The easier walk gave the dogs a break. I hauled the sled behind us while they flanked my sides for protection. I loved how even in the most exhausted state, their minds were sharp and still focused on our quest. Resting improved my mood and I felt a little giddy at the idea of seeing old Trade friends and acquiring some good finds in the Path.

In an hour's time, we had reached the edge of the forest. I led us out of the trees half a mile or so before the section of forest where I knew Beckett's house would be. Even though I had worked up the bravado to finally make good on my promise to visit the Trade Path, I wasn't ready to confront everything that cabin meant.

People meandered through the Collective, many with the good fortune of their trades bundled in their arms. In the center of town, now devoid of the festive decorations of Christmas, the Collective felt decidedly less cheery and inviting. No shiny bells or silky red ribbons, just utility and monotony.

When we arrived at the hitching post, I laid out a thermo-blanket for Tonk and Tilo. They were completely drained and collapsed into a heap of fur and paws. I considered leaving them with some hide, but decided they were better off sleeping. If I timed everything right, we would be camping at the base of the mountain tonight and headed back over the summit by mid-afternoon tomorrow. I had no interest in loitering in the Collective when the Path held more than just Traders that knew of my status. The stakes were higher now than ever before. Get in, get out, and go home.

With my newly-sewn satchel strapped across my chest, I took one deep, shaky breath before I stepped across the threshold and into the Path. My heart skipped a beat when I caught a glimpse of a Guard uniform. He turned in my direction and I held my breath. Relieved to find it wasn't him, I exhaled and steadied myself. Maybe Beckett wouldn't be here after all. I suppose it was arrogant to assume that he would be waiting with bated breath for me to return. Unapologetically, I'd left him alone and hurt, all for the sake of my pride. I wouldn't wait for me either.

I intended to visit Graham first and then make my way back until I had all the salt and grain I needed. No stopping to chat today, no giving in to the lure of the machine shop Traders' fancy wares. Just provisions, and maybe some cloth for a few new pillows, but that was it. I really enjoyed the little homey elements I had added to the cabin of late, so I figured some extra cushioning for the cot might be nice.

As much as I didn't want to veer from my plan, I couldn't ignore Servelle when I passed. The ashen color of her skin alarmed me. Sharp cheekbones jutted out from her hollowed face. Emptiness floated in place of a once buoyant demeanor. As we greeted, I worked to hide my shock at how frail she had become in the two months I had been absent.

"Cressenda, you're back." Her eyes were vacant and the smile she attempted fell just short of a grimace.

"I have some more peppermint today, if you need it. How is that baby of yours doing?"

She didn't answer me.

"Servelle, what's wrong? You look very ill." I didn't bother to conceal my concern.

Her lower lip trembled and tears poured from her eyes. Choking back a sob, she told me the facts as if she had rehearsed them a million times.

"Mercy...she died. A month ago. She was fine when I put her down to sleep. I found her in the morning. Her little body was so cold...she was gone." She choked back a sob. "The doctors had no explanation. She just died in her sleep, Cressenda. I wasn't even there to hold her." Servelle's narrow shoulders shook with the long, grief-filled cries that she fought to contain.

I pulled her close and brought her to the ground behind her trading table, shielding us from prying eyes. I held and rocked her the way my mother did when I was a child, unsure of any other way to console her. I knew how it felt to lose those you loved but I couldn't imagine the pain of losing a child. The very being that you gave flesh and bone, life and soul to, ripped from this world, had to dissolve the strongest of spirits.

Servelle stuffed her sorrow back inside and locked it down, turning to me to ask the only question I surely had no answer for.

"How will I live without her?"

I could only offer her what I knew of my own loss.

"You have to, Servelle. You are Mercy's mother, but you are also the mother to all the other beautiful babies you gave birth to, and they need to you keep the promise you made to them, to guide them through this life. They look to you for hope, for strength and security. Mercy will always be a part of you, nothing and no one can ever change that, but you can't give up. You can never give up, Servelle. You made a promise. You have to keep it."

She nodded, understanding what I didn't, even as the words passed through my lips. We sat a few more minutes on the ground, me tying teas into steeping bags and shoving them in her pockets despite her protests.

"Fine, I'll take one bag of grain, but only one, you hear me? You have to promise to drink the tea every day. Okay?" The tea couldn't take her pain away, but the ritual could be soothing and the herbs would be calming.

"Yes, I will. Thank you so much, Cressenda. You've always been such a good friend."

"I'll be back in two more months. Stay strong, Servelle."

Having given Servelle the majority of my tea leaves, I no longer had enough to trade for cloth. I dismissed the thought. More pillows would just take up space on my cot, anyway.

Graham's table sat at the very back of the Path. He didn't worry about trading and only came to the Path every month to escape the monotony of his elderly life. His table always held a hodgepodge of offerings, from general provisions to unusual knick-knacks that his wife created out of scraps of cloth and aluminum.

I smiled at him but his only response was to turn around and dig through a pile of who-knows-what behind him. Sifting through odds and ends scattered around his table, I considered that maybe he'd witnessed the commotion during my last visit, now choosing to shun me for being a troublemaker.

To my surprise, when he turned back to me, he held out the satchel that had been stolen by the ruffian Outlier.

"How did you...?"

"I'm an old man, I have my ways, and I'm not ratting anyone out. Now respect your elders and thank me." The smirk on his face coupled with his harsh commandment made me laugh, hard and sharp.

"Thank you, Graham. I'm sorry to say I don't have any resin for you today, but I can offer you some calendula."

"I'm just fine, but I'll take the calendula for the wife. Her skin has been itching, driving her crazy. And when she's crazy, she makes everyone else crazy. See anything you want?" He motioned to the smattering of items spread across the table.

One piece caught my eye. A wire heart, covered in white cloth, with a loop at the top. An ornament left over from the holiday season. It looked out of place against the rest of the pieces.

Graham knew immediately what I wanted. He didn't question my choice. Wrapping the delicate ornament in coarse brown paper, he shrugged and huffed as he handed it to me. Instead of placing it in my hand, he grabbed my arm and pulled me to him, whispering across the table.

"I saw what you did there, with Servelle. You're different. Something in you has changed. Don't let it go. If you love something, fight for it. Life is too short to play by the rules." He put a bag of salt in my hands and kissed my cheek.

With the stunning admission hanging over my head, he sent me on my way, back down the Path and into the throng of busy barterers. Stumbling blindly through blurred faces and jumbled bodies, I concentrated on the opening at the mouth of the Path. The warm air in the confined space made my mind slow. The intensity of the emotions from the afternoon's intimate interactions weighed me down. Each step I took toward the exit felt like wading through tree sap. Part of me wanted to give in, to become a prisoner—like an insect trapped in amber—in the life of the Affinity. But I knew it was just fatigue distorting my conscience.

I snapped back to reality and forced myself to move swiftly out the door. My head down and the hood of my coat up created a certain tunnel vision and I concentrated on the narrow vantage point until I felt the frozen air seeping in the opening of the Path hit my face. For a split second I turned my attention to the rows of Traders. When I looked up, Beckett stood directly in front of me. As I'd promised myself, I didn't address him, I didn't go to him, I didn't even acknowledge him.

The toe of my boot dropped just beyond the exit of the Trade Path, taunting me to continue, to walk away just like we'd agreed.

"Cressenda. Cressenda." He'd followed me.

No, damn it, we had an agreement. What the hell was he doing, yelling my name for the whole of Affinity to hear? Was he going to introduce me to council members next? Why couldn't he just let me leave with my dignity intact?

"Cressie!"

The endearing nickname stopped me in my tracks. Breathing heavily, I gave him the opportunity to catch me at the hitching post. The second moon sat low in the sky. A fresh wave of panic flooded through me knowing the sun would set in less than an hour.

"What are you doing?" I hissed, seething with anger. My barely bandaged heart ripped to pieces all over again at the nearness of him. "I came like I said I would. I'm fine. Don't make this harder than it already is."

"Cressie, please. Don't leave again. I've been waiting for you to come back. I started to think you never would." Beckett's smile stretched so far across his face it squeezed his whole face tight and hid the brilliance of his irises behind squinted joy.

"I have to. We've already had this conversation. It's not going to be any different the second time around."

"I can't take it. I'm miserable without you. Come back, come stay with me. I'll find a way to make it work. Maybe I can get a special exception, maybe we can be Matched. I love you, Cressie."

"I love you, too, Beckett. I do. I just can't. I want to so badly it's all I've thought about since I got home. But I can't. My life isn't here, it's not in the Collective and it's not under the Affinity."

"Then I'm going with you," he stated matter-of-factly, as if this was a perfectly normal thing to announce. Like he had just said he preferred his tea without soy milk or that he was thinking of getting a new snowmobile.

"What? You can't do that. Don't be ridiculous. Look, I knew this was a bad idea. I have to go." I unlatched the boys from the spot where they were hitched and they ran to greet Beckett, all jumps and yips of excitement. I quieted them and attached their harnesses to the sled.

"I'm going with you. I'm ready. I've been ready since the day you left. My mobile has been packed every day, waiting for you to come. I'm going with you."

Rage shot out of me and I flung myself at Beckett's body. I shoved my hands against his massive chest, hurling anger at him with every word I spoke.

"You can't come with me. This is your life. You belong here. Don't say things you do not and cannot mean." I hated him in that moment for planting hope in my heart and teasing me with fantasies of a happy life together in the wild. I hated myself for letting the idea settle in my head for even a second.

He held me tight and quieted my outburst, squeezing me until I stopped struggling against the hope and despair warring inside of me. Until I stopped struggling against him and his love.

"I'm coming with you, Cressie. There's nothing here for me. I have no life here. Life is with you, it's in you, and I need to be with you. If that means becoming an Outlier, fine. I'm ready. I love you."

I stared at him for a long time, searching his face for trepidation or fear. I found none. What I saw in Beckett was only eager acceptance, a willingness to face the unknown and fight for happiness in a life that promised nothing but struggle and sacrifice. I saw love. And with love behind us, we could build our own world, and find the warmth that had evaded us both for so long.

I kissed him long and hard, dizzy with the high of what our future could be.

"Well," I whispered into his neck, placing a kiss next to his ear, "what are you waiting for? Let's go."

ABOUT THE AUTHOR

Annabelle is a Science Fiction and Urban Fantasy Romance author, that is, when she's not checking homework or begrudgingly cooking dinner. Wife, mother, and

creator of alternate worlds, Annabelle has a penchant for that which is outside the norm.

Her Sociology degree did nothing to progress her writing skills, but has given her the ability to construct worlds that exist only in her head and translate them passionately to the page. The time spent studying individuals, interpersonal relationships, and particularly, women, within the constraints of our society led to Annabelle's unabashed ability to talk about sex as it fits into our modern lives.

She's also the author/personality of The Bombshell Mommy at Vitacost.com, where she expounds her knowledge of being a vixen clad in sweatpants.

Proof

13436243R00109

Made in the USA
Charleston, SC
10 July 2012